The

Women

of

JIMANAC

Ophelia Finsen

Also by Ophelia Finsen

Lovers of Old Films
This is Living
Society of Lost Causes

ISBN: 978-0-9559923-4-6

The Women of Jimanac
Chapters

Part One
Trees in the City

The property owner's shirt felt like a body sauna. He tugged at the collar, loosened the tie and tried to get a little air down the back of his neck. It was the middle of the day and the heat was pulsating through Jimanac like a microwave. He wished he was lying in his office, bare feet on the desk and sweat covered hair flying back in the cooling breeze thrown out from the fan. At the very least they could have gone and stood under that tree, but the sun worshipper who had brought him out here seemed to have a personal vendetta against anything natural looking.

"My Daddy owns this block opposite yours, but it would seem you own the courtyard area between," the blonde spoke, snapping her mobile phone shut. Her afternoon shopping spree with friends had been finalised. "So there's nothing he can do technically speaking. But he gave me the whole of the third floor as a birthday present – my own flat in the centre of town. I've got a gorgeous balcony but I can't use it. It's shadowed over by that thing all the time!" She pouted and pointed accusingly at the old, well-established tree that was the cause of this midday meeting.

The property owner was staring at the crown of her head. Her roots, dark brown, were starting to show. She wasn't a real blonde. He sourly thought how she would be clattering off in her pink stilettos to one of the exclusive hair saloons some day soon to get that problem fixed.

"Look, I don't know what you expect me to do. My tenants like the green area."

Are you completely stupid? the blonde, Anna Pearce, thought sulkily as she stared at the property agent. He had probably been attractive once, but his stomach was beginning to fall out of control. Middle age was creeping up from behind as it did and he hadn't taken the precautions. It was sad how people let themselves go; an exhausted sigh of defeat and a slackening of the belt. When she reached that age, she was damned if she wouldn't look more than a day over twenty-five.

"Well," she smiled at him, batting her extended eyelashes. Men needed smiles and reassurance to do anything. She had enough experience now to know how to get her own way with any breed of man. "This is the centre of Jimanac. The location is perfect, but there's always been a problem for me. I can't get a good off-road parking space for my little convertible. I know the other tenants in Daddy's block would pay generously for a parking space right outside their front door. You'd make a packet renting out spaces." She clasped his hands in hers and watched his eyes melt. The deal was done.

Anna and her shopping companion laughed about the matter later that day over cappuccinos. How easy it was to get your own way! Finishing coffee, stubbing out slender cigarettes, they flounced out of the sleek coffee shop to the next boutique, handbags full of little pieces of plastic that weren't, as Anna would say to her acquaintances and close friends, for amateurs.

The following morning the workmen arrived to tear down the green space and begin work on the new parking area. Anna Pearce - silk dipped earplugs in place to keep out most of the noise - sipped on a low calorie shake and watched in satisfaction as the bulldozer dug up the quaint tiled footpaths. Two men had just started to remove the upper sections of the tree with chain saws.

A flash of red at the low corner signalled that her weird neighbour, the red-haired witch from the opposite block of tenants, had arrived. The woman walked up to one of the workmen and started talking to him. Anna couldn't hear because of the window and the earplugs.

Down on the pavement, Nerina Torres was furious to discover that her favourite tree was being butchered. She waved desperately at the fat workman for his attention, who in turn stared dumbly at her for a full minute before turning his chain saw off. "Why are you cutting down this tree?" she cried desperately at him. "There's nothing wrong with it. It's perfectly healthy."

The workman merely looked her up and down. Long hair, long dress, lots of necklaces and bangles. No one had said anything to him about possible tree-hugging hippie problems.

"Can I help you, miss?" the foreman walked over to the rather one-sided conversation, ushering Pedro away.

She turned to the man. "Yes, why is this tree being torn down? Have we no respect left for anything now? This tree has been here for over a century. It's amazing how it has survived up until now in the city. I see no point in what you're doing."

Hippies, the man thought to himself, but smiled politely regardless of his preconceived ideas. "This is my job. I have been employed to clear this area. It's called progress."

"Progress?" Nerina protested. "There's hardly any space here. You can't tell me you're going to try and squeeze another apartment block in here."

"We're certainly not. This area is marked up for a parking area."

A parking area? Cars? Nerina gazed over the green area, distraught. This had been her little sanctuary in the heart of the city. She originally came from the countryside, forced into the city for opportunities and work. It had been a begrudged move, and the only consolation had been that the flat she inherited from an old spinster aunt, reputed witch, overlooked a beautiful oasis of peace in the middle of the chaos. "But the tree," she started. "You can't tear down a part of the city, a part of yourself."

The man barely managed to stifle a sneer. "I don't live here; it's got nothing to do with me."

"But it's got everything to do with you," Nerina contradicted. "It's a part of the city, and you're a part of that as well. It's one big living organism. We're all made of the same atoms. Therefore I am the city, the city is me and I am this tree. You're not going to chop me up, are you?"

It was too much for his instilled sense of customer relations. The man laughed openly in her face. It was entertaining which nutcases the construction business brought out of retirement. At least it had been in the past, but the entertainment had worn off in the past few years, taken over by apathy. "I thought your lot died off in the 80s. Get out of here; you've been in the sun too long."

Nerina scowled at the foreman as he turned his back on her dismissively and wandered without thought into the dust-ridden heat of destruction. The tree in question shuddered as a man plunged a chainsaw into its wooden flesh, tearing at the natural fibres. Another tree fell in the name of progress and concrete. Progress was just a word they used to describe something else. Nerina felt civilisation had been going backwards for a long time.

Her eyes dropped to the ground as the tree shook violently, as if it was unable to control the agony caused by the chainsaw teeth. An offering of seeds sprayed out across the dirt, a desperate attempt to continue the species, soon to be trampled down and covered in concrete. Ducking down, she scooped up a heavy handful and hurried away to her flat.

Upstairs Nerina closed the door to her tiny balcony to keep out the choking dust that was coming up from the work site. She worked at her kitchen table for the rest of the morning, filling plant pots with moist earth and adding a seed to each. The tree would live on somehow. Even if it had to start over from the beginning.

The following days saw the removal of the carnage, broken tiles, torn limbs and trunks tossed into city council skips. The men cleared the area, levelled it off and brought in the concrete trucks. A thick layer of concrete was poured out between the two buildings, stifling out all chances of life on that little patch of dirt in Jimanac. It dried quickly in the heat, and the spaces were quickly marked out and bought by rich locals. Anna Pearce was the first to bring her car onto the site, and sat gleefully on her balcony staring down at her little red convertible. She bought herself a large sun lounger, setting it up on her balcony. She had an important party at the weekend and needed a stunning suntan. It was to mark the start of her husband hunting and she wanted to make a good impression. She would sunbathe in the nude out on her balcony; strap lines were like stretch marks and body hair – a big no. If the perverts wanted to look, that was their problem.

On the other side of the concrete-strangled air Nerina set her precious plant pots out on her balcony in direct reach of the sunlight. Under the surface of the soil the seeds soaked up the heat and life began to emerge. The weeks passed by and fresh green shoots appeared, reaching up for the glowing orb of the sun. Window boxes full of herbs of and flowers appeared at each of Nerina's windows, and the air around her flat seemed to clear a little.

By the middle of August it was so hot during the middle of the day that the city seemed to melt to a halt. The electricity usage boomed as fridges were fighting to keep their contents chilled, and a million electric fans were switched on to cool sweating brows.

It was nearing noon when Anna Pearce had her first attack. She could almost hear her skin sizzling in the heat, too hot to touch. Something seemed to break in her mind, and when she opened her eyes, her vision lurched up in front of her. Disorientated, she sat up, gasping. She felt light-headed. Hot air flooded into her lungs. She could not breathe. Her legs felt weak, she was not sure she could make it into her flat. She wished there was a little shade out here, glancing at the blue intense space where the tree had once been.

Daddy's private doctor was promptly called to the daughter's flat. He was a man of fifty something years, who had seen the worst of the rich's indulgences. Anna was sat on the leather sofa in her living room, all the blinds closed and the air conditioning on full power as he handed her a glass of water.

"And you say you're out on the balcony every day?"

"Yes, virtually everyday. I don't want the tan to fade. You wouldn't believe the competition." She looked up at the doctor through her sunglasses – her eyes had become incredibly sensitive to light all of a sudden. "Everyone needs a little sunshine."

"Little being the operative word," the doctor muttered. "You've been out in the sun too long, quite simply," he informed her, looked at the over-tanned skin, the snake-skin flaking effect beginning to appear here and there. She was like a desert. "And you're not using a high enough factor sun cream," he added, shaking the bottle at her. "I very much doubt you top up regularly enough. Plus you are very dehydrated. If your father hadn't insisted and sent a private nurse, I would be sending you to hospital."

"Daddy can't afford any gossip right now."

"Well, I want you to stay out of the sun for several days. Get a lot of liquids into you. And I want you to get that mole on your shin checked out."

"What mole? I've only got a little birthmark there, barely a freckle," Anna scoffed. Leaning slowly forward, she peered at the sleek bronzed leg the doctor had referred to. At least it had just been a little birthmark. Now it looked like a growing clump of dark brown bubbles coming out of her leg. Panic tightened her throat. "That wasn't there last time I looked!"

"These things can come up quickly. There's a lot of harmful rays in the sun. You really must cut back on your sunbathing. And definitely not at noon. You..." The doorbell interrupted the lecture. The doctor left Anna for a minute, to let the nurse into the apartment. They had a short technical conversation which Anna did not have the concentration to follow. Worried glances were shot in her direction. The nurse, much younger than Anna had been expecting, gave a sharp nod and said she would talk to Anna about it.

"Anna, I'm going to leave you with Nurse Cortez now," the doctor returned, talking to her as if she was hard of hearing. "You drink plenty of water and get some rest. Nurse Cortez will take you to the hospital and we'll get that mole tested tomorrow."

Anna's eyes widened. "That soon?"

"No point in hanging about."

Much to the disappointment of the socially inept city banker on the top floor, Anna Pearce did not appear on her balcony during the following month, let alone strip off. No one saw Anna apart from

Nurse Cortez, who had moved into the flat, and her father, who visited now and then. With the blinds frequently closed, she sat in her room and gazed out through the chinks at the sunlit world from the safety of her shadows.

The strange mole, sadly the first of many, had been removed from her leg and tested. The horrific day when the doctors had confirmed it was indeed cancer still echoed maliciously in her head. She had skin cancer. Even after the weeks of treatment, the operations and the deterioration of her skin, it was still hard to comprehend. Wasn't she too young, too indestructible for all this? Clearly not. So she sat in her chair by the window, gazing resentfully out at the car park she dared not show her diseased body in, and wished that she had never asked for the tree to be cut down.

Anna could have coped physically with more than she did, but something shut down in the girl's mind that day cancer was declared, and from then on she sat like an emaciated cripple swathed in layers of clothing, refusing to do anything. Nurse Cortez not only saw to all of Anna's medical needs, but became housekeeper too, with a part time nurse taking over at weekends to give her a much-needed rest from the oppressive mood of the apartment.

Anna's mood was breaking the nurse's own general optimistic outlook and steady nerves. When Nerina bumped into Nurse Cortez one midday morning, she looked as though her mind had finally gone. The paper shopping bag had burst, setting free a cascade of oranges that had rolled out across the pavement. The nurse stood and robotically counted the oranges, but made no effort to retrieve them.

"Are you all right?"

Nurse Cortez snapped out of her trance and shook her head to wake up. A woman with long red hair was crouched on the pavement picking up oranges. She glanced up at the nurse and raised her eyebrows, still waiting for an answer.

"Oh, yes, thank you," she responded in a daze, picking up the remains of the bag that still contained a bunch of celery and a bag of prunes. "I'm just a bit frazzled by work. Then the bag breaks…"

Nerina smiled sympathetically. "Well, have you got far to go with all these?"

"No, just in here." She pointed at the door she was stood beside.

On the way up in the lift, Nerina studied the woman's face. "Tell me, what do you work with?"

"I'm a nurse."

"Oh, I understand now. I've read about how stressful that profession can be. The long hours, staff shortages…"

"Awkward patients." Nurse Cortez added with a sigh.

"Which hospital do you work at?"

"I don't. I'm a private nurse. I stay at people's homes and help them recuperate. I've just got the one patient at the moment. I live here."

The lift doors separated and they stepped out into a small hall that served as entrance to the only flat on the entire floor. Unlocking the door, the nurse walked in first, gesturing to a small table against the wall. "You've been very kind. If you can just leave them there, I will deal with them later."

The phone started ringing somewhere in the depths of the flat. Nurse Cortez excused herself over her shoulder, forgetting the front door and Nerina, running to answer the telephone.

Nerina gazed at her surroundings, left alone in this giant empty shell. There was a lot of potential but not much had been done. It felt very minimalistic here. The furniture looked very expensive, and whilst very well crafted, it did not seem to fill the flat. There was an overall feeling of emptiness and death.

"Who are you?"

Nerina jumped, surprised to discover that a heap of clothes on a chair across the room was actually a person. Clothes hung baggily on the skeletal frame, covering over all but hands and face. The girl, at least she presumed the figure was a girl judging by the voice, the hair or what was left of it, but for that, the sheer fleshless quality of the body suggested that little more than a wretch would have been a fitting description.

"My name is Nerina Torres," she introduced herself. "Your nurse dropped some shopping outside and I helped her carry it up here."

The girl's eyes, void of makeup and eyelashes, narrowed slightly as she examined Nerina's long skirts, the necklaces and the lightly tanned arms on display. No worries of faulty skin there. No weak gene in the family. She already knew who the woman was – she had recognised her as the witch from the other building – but she had not known her name up until this point.

"And what is it you do?"

"You mean my profession?" Nerina faltered. This girl couldn't have been more than twenty-five but there was something about her manner that made her feel like she was talking to a petulant old woman. "I work with aromatherapy, herbal healing…"

"The wonder of nature," Anna muttered, looking back out of the window. "I've seen you before. You live on the other side of the courtyard."

Nerina smiled dryly. "Well, these days it's the other side of the car park, but yes, that's where I live."

There was a long, uncomfortable moment of silence. Far in the background the sound of Nurse Cortez's voice dealt with unwelcome questions on the telephone. Anna looked back at Nerina. "I got them to tear down that tree," she suddenly blurted out, not sure where this sudden desperate need to confess originated from. She had seen the witch, Nerina, scrabble in the dirt when the workmen hadn't been looking. She had taken something with her, fistfuls of something. Then the seedling trees had appeared on the opposing balcony.

Nerina was not surprised. "Well, I am sure you had your reasons."

"I wanted to sunbathe on my balcony."

"Why aren't you out there now, then?"

"I had to give it up."

"Thanks again for your help," Nurse Cortez bustled back into the room, all smiles and pretension that the telephone conversation had not just happened. She ignored the icy atmosphere, putting it down to another one of Anna's indulgent tantrums.

"It was no problem," Nerina assured her. "I've got to get going now. Goodbye."

Anna was very quiet for the rest of the day, much to Nurse Cortez's relief. She sat at her window and stared at where the tree had once stood. That bloody tree. Before it had been cut down, she had been forced to drive out to the country club to sunbathe. She had never been out in the sun that long, for there were always friends and male distractions, lunches to eat indoors and games of tennis to be played. Plus the long drive out there. The tree's execution had cut out all of that, and she had rolled straight from bed to the balcony where she had lain and roasted without distraction, frequently falling asleep. That damned tree. If she hadn't cut it down, none of this would have happened.

The next morning Nurse Cortez was woken by angry shouting. She lay still for a moment; the pillow cover stuck to the side of her face, and wondered where she was. Disorientated, she gazed across at the far wall, thinking this was not her home. Her memory started to function and she realised, with that sinking feeling everyone goes through on the approach to a Monday, that she was still working at Anna Pearce's home. Anna was shouting.

Already dressed in her uniform, because Anna demanded attention at all hours of the day, Nurse Cortez staggered out of her small bed and into the corridor. She moved down the length of the flat, listening to her name on repeat, and wondering what had happened now. As she passed the kitchen, she noticed that it was not even seven in the morning yet.

She stopped when she saw where Anna was. The balcony doors were wrenched open, after weeks of lock down, and Anna, dressed in her baggy shirts and trousers, sunglasses shielding her eyes from the harshness of the full blast of light, was out on the balcony, pointing at something in the far corner.

"How did this get here?"

"What?" The nurse walked up to the balcony and peered out. There was a small sapling growing in a brightly coloured pot. It was the first real plant she had seen in Anna's extensive apartment. "I don't know, I've never seen it before."

Anna looked sharply across the car park to the opposing balcony on her level. She could not see Nerina the witch today, but she could see the multitude of pots with plants stood out on the balcony. "She put it here," she accused. "When she found out it was me who had the tree cut down, she came back at night and broke in."

"No one came into the flat last night," Nurse Cortez sighed, her patience wearing thin. "The flat is locked, you know that. Your father installed a very good security system."

"Well, maybe she sneaked it in when she helped you carry those things up."

"You're being ridiculous," Cortez informed her, turning to go to the kitchen and make some coffee.

Anna knew Nerina could not have put the plant there yesterday though; she was just desperately searching for an explanation, for someone to blame. She had watched Nerina closely the whole time she had been in the flat. The young tree seemed to have appeared there quite illogically. It was impossible, not only the fact that it had seemingly transported itself to a balcony three storeys up, but also that it was growing in her glass mosaic punchbowl, the one that had been stuffed in the back of one of her cupboards.

Half an hour later, when Nurse Cortez returned to the balcony, Anna was still standing there.

"Look, do you want me to get rid of it?"

Anna looked over at her nurse. She had had the area cleared of all greenery, all natural features that got in the way, but the tree had somehow made it here anyway.

"No, leave it where it is."

Part Two
A Legendary Travel Writer

The mud-splashed, clay-red leather boot moved out of the car to the pavement. Its mate, equally grubby and in need of a wash, left the car a second later. The long skirts, turquoise blue and crumpled from the long drive, came cascading down to the ankles, hiding the shin length of the boots. The doorman at the elite hotel stood and watched in awe as the porter ran down to drive the guest's car to the car park in the basement of the hotel. The sole passenger of the red vehicle looked over the top of her round sunglasses as the porter took her car keys. She took a scruffy moss green hold all off the back seat and slung it over her shoulder before her car was driven away. That was the kind of service you got at the good hotels. It was something she had missed the past couple of months; forced to live in a multitude of some of the most basic youth hostels for the sake of her assignment. Thankfully, the last sentence was now written, the final make shift shower tested. She was moving on to better things.

The doorman smiled politely, opening the door to let her pass into the dignified lobby of one of Jimanac's most prestigious hotels. As the woman disappeared into the cool, air-conditioned interior, another guest departed. The man looked over his shoulder and watched the stranger he had just brushed past walk over to reception. He was so involved in unashamedly staring at her that he would have walked straight into the door if it had not been for the doorman.

"I'm sure I've seen her somewhere before."

"Probably on the back of a book, Sir," the doorman responded knowledgeably. "That was Terri Sanchez, the travel writer."

"The one from Brazil?"

The doorman nodded proudly as if he was the publishing genius that had discovered her.

In truth, unbeknown to the vast majority of the world, the woman was all that and more. Terri Sanchez was little more than a pseudonym, developed for her second writing career as a non-fiction storyteller of her travels across the world. A woman who told tales of her adventures, meetings with eccentrics and experiences of different cultures, published in well-read paperbacks and glossy books. All complete with photographs for the armchair traveller who would never get beyond the package holiday destination. She was not from Brazil either, but the myth of Terri Sanchez's roots had come about during a misunderstanding at an interview when she had spoken Portuguese, in which she was fluent since extensive travels in the Amazon country.

Despite the depth of experiences and the long list of publications, Terri Sanchez was essentially little more than a name. She was also Rosita Almodez, an award-winning short story novelist living in France (allegedly); and her true and original identity – Aria Fernandez. Aria had already written many practical travel guides for countries across the world and would certainly continue to stock the shelves in the travel section in bookshops worldwide for many years to come. Her books were filled with reviews and tips on the best hotels, restaurants, cafes, sights and transport methods.

Of the people acquainted with her various works, a few were aware of a common mind behind two of the names. Only one knew that all three were the product of two busy hands on a laptop keypad.

Initially Aria had not wanted to come to Jimanac. She had immediately turned down the assignment when she learned where it was to be based. Yet the publisher was adamant that she would write chapter three of the new guide book to Jimanac. The concept was for a compilation written by nationals, who would add their own view and advice on an aspect of living in and visiting Jimanac. It would be translated into seven languages initially. It would boost the tourist industry. Everyone would be heroes.

Aria was a well-known name within the travel guide industry, and it was a simple must that she would be included in the definitive guide to a major city in her home country. Her publisher had eventually persuaded her with a large payment and promises of a good hotel, which he had not fallen short of. He thought he understood her perfectly; that she was just holding out to earn a few more hundred than her colleges on her book. With her name she could do that too. But it was not the money that had made her hesitant. It was Jimanac.

Aria was fiercely independent. She had travelled all over the world several times, and if there was anyone who knew about surviving human civilisation, it was she. Aria could and had looked after herself through many dire situations, and was least in need of a man in that respect of all womankind. She spoke five languages fluently, another four at a reasonable level to get by, and got along easily with people. Yet she was by definition a loner, drifting from one place to the next with her laptop and sparse permanent belongings. She tended to sell off what she could, even down to basic clothing, when she was to leave a country, and would purchase replacements when she arrived at her next destination. She was good at being permanently on the move. She ought to be, she had been doing it for the past eleven years.

There was no permanent address with her name posted on the door. Much of her correspondence went via the publishers. She had been travelling that long that her work colleges had never stopped and thought that maybe once she had roots, perhaps once she had a home.

She set her sunglasses down on the clean glass tabletop as the waiter brought her a cup of hot steaming coffee. Aria lent back in her chair and listened to the sound of the ceiling fans rotating through the chilled air. It had been eleven years since she had last been in Jimanac. New shops and businesses had appeared, buildings had been torn down and a lot of roads had been added. This coffee house had not existed back then, but somehow the streets had not changed. The soul of the city was pretty much as she remembered, almost as if someone had set it to pause whilst she had been away. It was very strange to be back.

"Why, hello there." A man in a business suit poured himself into the chair opposite her, flashing a smile as if he knew what she wanted. "I always come here after work; I know all the regulars, and I've never seen you before."

Aria forced a limp smile and pushed his coffee cup back as he leaned in for the kill he did not have the personality to make. "That's because I've never been here before, sweetheart," she responded, speaking to him on the level he had approached her. "And I don't intend seeing this coffee house or you again."

The man lent away from her as if she was contagious, the smile dropping off his face like a landslide. He grunted, unable to think of a good response. Picking up his coffee, he wandered off, muttering something about lesbians to console his pride.

Aria slung a lazy arm over the back of her chair, finished her coffee and brushed loose black hair back over her ear. The more you travelled, the smaller the world became. Perhaps it had come too small for her. She had been everywhere, visited literally every country in the world and had a cupboard full of photographs stored at one of her publishers. Maybe it was time for a change; perhaps she ought to stop moving before the world became so small it disappeared. Staying in one place; the normality and repetition of day-to-day routine had originally been what had driven her onto the travel route.

She glanced up as the man with the coffee shared a joke with another man, and they glanced in her direction. It was almost terrifying how often you came upon the same characters. Men who thought a patronising smile would catch her attention, and in failure threw words of sexuality about like accusations. Occasionally she had indulged herself in short lived affairs in exotic countries when she was there long enough to sift through the slime to the real gems, but nothing that could ever last enough to calm her itching feet. There was always something new to see, and there were few that could really tolerate her lifestyle. Most gave up on her. There were a couple she had been back to a few times: a fisherman in Scotland, and a banker in Alaska, but she doubted they would still be available the next time she visited on assignment. They were all at an age now when they ought to be settling down.

"More coffee?"

"Yes, please." Aria nudged her cup across the table slightly.

The waiter poured until the cup was three quarters full, the coffee swirling in its porcelain confines. He lifted up the coffee jug and moved to go before stopping and peering quizzically at Aria's face. "Don't I know you?"

"I don't think so," Aria shook her head, letting her black hair fall around her face to shield her features. She did not meet the waiter's gaze. "I don't live here."

"Jesus Christ!" the waiter burst out, a spark of memory lighting up. "Aria Fernandez, it is you, isn't it? Your hair's a damn sight longer and you've lost some weight – that's why I didn't recognise you straight away. It's Jimmy," he said, gesturing at himself. "Remember?"

She smiled weakly, meeting his eye for the first time. Jimmy was her opposite. A lot less hair and a lot more weight. "Sure."

"Christ, it must be ten years since I last saw you."

"Eleven."

"Right," he nodded, the conversation dying off. "So, what are you doing back here?"

"Work."

"You got a job in Jimanac? You moving back?"

"No, just passing through."

"Just passing through," he echoed. "Hoping no one would notice, I'll guess. We never heard a word from you, not even Casar. You just packed your bags and…"

"Like you said, it was eleven years ago," Aria interrupted. This was one of the reasons she had not returned to Jimanac once in all that time.

"Water under the bridge," Jimmy assured her. "We've all moved on, got on with our lives. Doesn't mean we didn't wonder what happened to you. You doing all right? Where you living now?"

She shrugged. "Wherever my work takes me. I travel a lot."

"Yeah? I remember you talked a lot about travelling before you left." He paused, running something silently over in his mind. "Are you going to see Casar whilst you're here?"

"I don't think so. I'm not here that long and I don't have time to try and track him down."

"He lives just around the corner."

Damn. Aria silently cursed the news.

"Take the first left, and go to number twenty-eight. You'll see his name on the intercom. Casar did well for himself. He's a lawyer now. You should go and see him, just say hi or whatever. He does wonder sometimes. We all do. It's good to know you're all right."

"I'll do that." She really didn't want to.

Everything was just as Jimmy had described. Aria gazed up at the list of names, wondering why she was here. It was probably curiosity, something she had allowed to lie dormant in her subconscious these past eleven years.

She found Casar's handwriting amongst the scraps of scrawl pushed in beside buttons. She thought about buzzing up, but someone had left the main door open, and she didn't know what she would say to the intercom. It would be easier to take this face to face. It had been a long time since she had felt this uncertain.

Casar lived on the third floor. His front door was red, the paint looked quite fresh. He always had liked things to be neat and tidy. Taking a deep breath and praying he would not be home, Aria raised her hand and rapped her knuckles against the hard wood.

Two seconds of silence dragged out like weeks of starvation. Someone came to the door, unlocked it and opened it. A man stood and stared at her blankly. "Yes, can I help you?"

He was older, tired, with noticeable bags under the eyes. Grey hairs were beginning to appear in his once luscious black hair. But it was still Casar; his eyes were just as she remembered them. How old must he be now? Thirty-eight if her memory was correct. He was mature, finally grown up, even wearing a suit, which she had never expected to see.

When she had known him, he had been a scruffy law student threatening to become an environmental activist after his studies were complete. A skinny, passionate man who held firm to his beliefs and was aggressively loyal to the family.

"Look, I'm just stopping by to say hello, let you know I'm OK," she started, her mind off balance as if she had never been away. This was eleven years too late and she sounded a fool blurting everything out like this, but it was too late. "Jimmy told me you lived here."

"Jimmy told you…" he murmured, peering at her closely. "Aria?" he suddenly realised, his exhausted eyes widening in shock. "Is that actually you?"

She could not help but smile. "Yes."

"You disappeared, just left. We had no idea…" he broke off. "It's been a while. Do you want to come in?"

"Well, I can't stay long," she lied, following him into the flat. Slipping past him, she wandered into a large living room. Everything looked clean and new here; fresh sunlight coming in through the window. She wondered how he had managed to create this calm serene atmosphere in the middle of the rush of Jimanac. Casar had done well for himself. To think, if she had not left that day, she would be living here. She might be…

"Who's this?"

Aria turned to discover a woman standing in the hall doorway, hands on hips and a sour look on her face. It was an expression of immediate distaste, and perhaps jealously. The two women surveyed each other in a cold manner. They were about the same age, but it looked as though they had lived very different lives. This woman looked older than Aria, tired, bored with life, frustrated by stagnation perhaps. Her plain face was worn, her short hair untidy. The years had put on a few rings of flab around her waist and hips.

"Anita, darling," Casar turned innocently to the woman with a smile on his face. "This is Aria Fernandez. She just turned up on the doorstep." He looked back at Aria. "And this is Anita, my wife."

His wife. She did not know why she was quite so surprised to learn he had married. Casar had always had that homely streak in him, a desperate longing for the domestic life. It had been eleven years; he was not expected to mourn her forever. Besides, that had been half the reason for her departure – Casar hadn't been quite what she wanted with her life.

"Aria Fernandez." The wife mulled over the name, then recognition came into her eyes. A smile of satisfaction touched her lips. So the old ex fiancée who had run away in childish terror had come back to see what she had missed out on. "Yes, I heard about you. You left a couple of months before I met Casar."

"I'm glad to see you are settled." Aria spoke, gazing curiously at Anita for another moment before looking back at Casar. "I really only came to say hello; that I'm all right…"

"Don't you think you should apologise?" Anita snapped. "You ran out on him."

Casar shuffled awkwardly. He looked embarrassed. "That was a long time ago."

"Besides, you should be thanking me. If I hadn't had run out..." Aria stopped. "I just dropped by to say hello. Maybe it was a mistake. But you're well?"

"Yes," Casar perked up. "I've been married almost ten years to Anita. I have a good job, we have a son."

"And what about you? Did you ever settle down?" Anita questioned harshly, stepping territorially into the room.

She did not understand why this woman was so hostile. They had never met, and as everyone kept saying, it had all happened a long time ago. "I travel a lot," Aria responded, "For my work."

"Really?" The acid tone in Anita's voice dropped in the pH level. "Where have you been?"

"Oh, you know, most countries," Aria responded absently. The thrill of being 'abroad' had dissolved a long time ago for her. The world was her country now, no one place her home. "It's my work; I write travel guides."

"Oh." Anita's gaze dropped. Perhaps she was a little taken aback. The crazy girl she had only heard rumours and myths of, like an eccentric urban legend, was not only real but seemed to be surviving very nicely. It was certainly a more exciting life than her housewife role. She had never really travelled, a few holidays to the coast, but that was all. She had stayed in Jimanac all her life. Cleaning up the vomit from her son's bed this morning, two loads of washing for the laundry room, dusting, cooking... the list of chores was endless.

"But you must feel very rootless. Don't you wish to belong somewhere?"

Aria gazed at Casar. He had changed since she had known him. The activism, the hunger for the world had died off. He was at that age they were getting to. Everyone was supposed to settle down; many already had. Aria was different, she probably always would be. A whisper of a legend. Another way of living. "You can't have everything."

"I suppose," Casar sighed, merely agreeing with her because he knew that it would not be possible for him to persuade Aria away from her very definite opinions. He never had been able to. "But if you're happy, then that's all that matters."

"I enjoy my life," Aria assured him, taking one last glance at the pristine living room and the tired circles around Anita's worn face. The things that might have been. "I just thought I ought to say hello. And goodbye. Properly this time. I have to go to a meeting now."

"Right, of course," Casar nodded, full of domestic, middle aged compliance. "I suppose the life of a writer is very busy."

"Oh, it is," Aria agreed, walking to the door. Especially if you are three writers.

"Thanks for stopping by. It's good to know…"

Aria turned in the open doorway. Anita was slumped in the background, pondering on daydreams, waiting until the door would close and Aria would disappear from their lives. Permanently. Casar, with his back to his second choice for a wife, stared at Aria, almost with some unexplained urgency. It had been a long time, but perhaps not long enough for some feelings.

Aria lowered her eyes. "Goodbye Casar."

She did not wait for a response, heading quickly down the staircase. Perhaps it had been good to come here. There had been moments when she had been sleeping rough in the jungle, or waiting for a midnight train, when she wondered if she had made a mistake. When her confidence had faltered. She had no regrets from that choice. It had been the right thing to do.

Full of fresh spirit and eagerness, she walked swiftly down the street. Onwards to the next coffee shop. She would get her article researched and written in the next two days, then she would move on. Casar had awakened her need to travel, to get out of Jimanac again. Who knew where she would be next week? Suddenly the world was a very big place again.

Part Three
Just Got to Get Out of This Place

Renata pulled the elastic hair band out of her hair and flicked it across the office at Malcolm's fat, sagging backside. His arse looked like a pair of deflated water balloons, liquid sloshing around in the bottom halves. Malcolm let out an irritated cry, slapped his rump as if something had bitten him, and glanced around. Renata let out a bored sigh and turned back to her computer. When had living become so dull? Nothing had changed, but during the past few months things had been getting her down. The noise, the people, the rush on the streets every morning to work, the forced smiles and laughs covering over so many frustrations. The stuffy atmosphere in this office. The city was enduring one of its worst heat waves to date and the effect was stifling.

She pulled off her cardigan as she felt the first trickle of sweat run down her neck. She really shouldn't have thrown away her hair band. Now her hair was loose it gave an insulation to her neck that she didn't need.

She was tired with life. Unbelievable, she was not even thirty yet. She supposed she needed a change, to get out, to do something to shake things up a bit. She needed to get back to basics, to feel alive again. This state of mind was the curse of consciousness. If only she was an animal. She wouldn't have to think. She wouldn't be able to think. She eased her feet out of her shoes, smiling as she flexed her bare toes. That felt a little better.

Renata looked up as she heard the department manager's voice as he stepped out of the lift. He looked like a film star, sauntering through the office, flashing smiles at Maria and Cindy and ignoring everyone else. Renata felt she was going mad. Her eyes drifted back to the lift. She had to get out of here.

Forgetting her shoes, she wandered over to the lift, hoping no one would see her. Paranoia burned through her skin, and she began to feel uncomfortably hot. Frustrated by everything. They always said life was beautiful, but she had seen nothing but a grey monotony for so long. A strange urge came upon her, something she could not explain, and in years to come she would be as equally baffled. It was out of character, it would never be repeated, but her mind was near to breaking point and something had to give. Unbuttoning her blouse, she tossed it onto the photocopier before stepping into the lift.

The security guard's eyes widened in a mix of shock and horror as the lift on ground floor opened and a woman stepped out in only her underwear – skirt and petticoat lying in the lift behind her. "Er, Miss…" he started awkwardly as she headed towards the exit. He really wasn't sure what to say. This kind of thing hadn't been covered in the training course. He jumped up from his chair and hurried over to the exit through which the woman had just departed. A shriek from the street went up as he stepped out onto the pavement in time to see Renata streaking down the road, her pale, chubby backside wobbling along behind her.

Fifteen minutes later, after a thousand car horn honks, cheers and jeers, clapping, shielded eyes and looks of slapped shock, Renata was picked up by a blushing policeman outside a distinguished law firm. She was dancing in the fountain and laughing, oblivious to the bemused but entertained group of Japanese tourists on the other side of the road who were taking photographs. A large dark grey blanket was thrown around her shoulders by the policemen and she was lead dripping wet with a large, relieved smile on her face, to the car.

By ten o'clock she was sitting in an interview room at an inner city police station. She was now wearing an oversized blue shirt and a very baggy pair of shorts she had to hold on to so that they would not fall down around her ankles. Both items were old unwanted police uniform that they had found to put her in until her mother arrived with more suitable attire.

After several hours in police custody, she was eventually released with a warning. Her mother had arrived with trousers and a very large jumper – clothes that concealed every inch of her body with utter thoroughness. Dressed in clothes that she had not worn since that skiing trip to the mountains five years ago, she had driven home with her mother.

Her mother had been surprisingly calm, perhaps the shock had yet to register, and had given her daughter a bemused look as they left the police station, as if to say 'are we really related?'

"Why did you want to do such a thing?" the elder woman asked as she parked the car outside Renata's block.

Renata shrugged her shoulders. "I suddenly felt like it. I felt so tired of everything that I just had to… I just had to shake things up a bit."

"Yes, but did you really have to shake them about in the centre of town?"

She had needed to do it, although she could not really explain it any better, even to herself. She had been born into the city – a beautiful gem in the riches of this metropolis, but over the years she had become dull and smothered by pollution, disappointment and car fumes. In that spontaneous moment she had ripped off the dirt and emerged as a diamond. Naturally, it was not a method of therapy she would recommend for others, and Renata would never do it again but that in moment dancing in the fountain she had felt truly free.

The following morning was soon drained of ideology when she caught sight of her photograph in the morning newspaper. It was front-page material, very little text, but there she was, her massive bottom glowing brightly like two lumps of mozzarella in the black and white photograph. Renata blushed despite the fact that she was at home alone. At least the paper had done her the courtesy of printing a photo of her turning away from the camera, so as to save most of her dignity, she supposed, but even so, it was all very humiliating. And as she looked at the kitchen clock she realised it was going to get a lot worse before it got better. She was going to have to go to work. And if she did not go today, she would only have to face them another day. It was better to get it over with.

In the lobby to her workplace the security guard seemed more alert than usual, tipping his hat in her direction as she walked past. Renata immediately turned her eyes to the floor and hurried to the lift. There were eight people going up, two with newspapers. Renata cringed every time she heard the crinkle of paper, a page turning, catching sight of *that* photograph. She felt as though they were all staring at her.

The lift doors opened and she stepped out into her workplace. They must have been waiting for her, and they must have arrived to work especially early that morning, because she was the last one in the office and she was five minutes early. Someone hissed 'Renata's here' and a silence came down upon the office, papers rustling, people rushing to the side of the room. A tape cassette player was switched on and stripper music blared out. A mix of cheering and laughing ripped out through the large room and Renata, all alone at the head of it, went bright red.

Someone had put a small electric fan on her desk with a note attached saying 'In case you get too hot again'. She was embarrassed by the further recognition of that thing she had done, but later in the day, when the sun-powered heat was at its strongest, she was grateful for the anonymous gift.

Across the room she heard conversations throughout the day dissecting her behaviour. It was the most attention she had ever had, and she did not care for it.

"It's such a sad, attention-seeking stunt," Cindy added to the discussion she was involved in with Maria and the section manager.

"Oh, I don't know," he commented, staring at Maria's skirt. "A friend of mine said that it was a great piece of art, what she did. An expression of innocence, simple joys in a chaotic world."

Maria took the pen she was sucking out of her mouth and laughed. "What, you hang around with art professors now?"

"Well, no," the boss started awkwardly. "He runs a pornography shop. But it's very high class stuff."

Cindy sniggered. "I suppose he'll be wanting to buy the rights. Although I don't know why she did it. It's not like she's got anything worth flashing."

Renata slumped in front of her computer and hoped no one would notice her ever again.

"I saw your picture in the paper." Malcolm stopped by her desk, an arm full of photocopying in one hand and a plastic cup of water in the other. "Black and white photography always looks very atmospheric. Of course, it's not the best photograph of the bunch. There's a lot more on the Internet when you look."

Renata's eyes widened in horror. The Internet? Already? Not even twenty-four hours had past. "You've been searching on the Internet?"

Malcolm reddened. "It's just what I heard," he muttered, hurrying away to his desk.

Renata closed her eyes and prayed for a localised earthquake that would tear this building down and bury her alive. She really should have thought about the consequences. Spontaneity did not pay.

She worked late that day to give the majority of employees chance to leave for home before she had to show her face away from the computer. In the lift, apart from Renata, there was only Joel. He was a notoriously quiet man who stared at anything other than people. He was currently staring at his shoes. He had unbelievably thick lenses in his glasses; it reminded her of her old grandfather before he had passed away.

"I really admire you," Joel unexpectedly burst out, suddenly looking her straight in the eye – a jolting movement that made Renata stagger back in embarrassment, realising she had been staring at him like a new found bug pinned out under a microscope.

"What you did yesterday, to have the guts to just get out there and do, regardless of what anyone else might think or say. Spontaneity, that's really it, isn't it? The courage to actually live. It was a really beautiful gesture."

Renata wrinkled her nose. "It's not all it's cracked up to be."

Her mortification only continued to grow when she got home that evening. The post had arrived in her absence, including two fan letters from local perverts (where had they got her address from?); a large, glossy black and white print from the newspaper photographer who had included a note thanking her for being the subject of one of his best pieces of work to date; and an official invitation to the Jimanac Nudist Society. Renata wailed in distress. She was neither nudist nor exhibitionist; no pornographic plaything nor artist's muse. Why were these people bothering her? Skipping her evening meal, she went straight to bed and indulged herself in a long session of self-pity.

The following weeks proved to be filled with some very curious events. Although they were unconnected to Renata, she could not help but wonder privately to herself if they were all born of the same origin.

The security guard at her building was seen to be sitting behind his desk less and less, instead moving around the lobby, nodding to people and genuinely smiling rather than the plastic thing handed out at training school for the security profession. He always gave Renata a little extra attention, and one day, as he trotted away back to the desk, his footsteps clicking extremely loudly against the polished stone floor, Renata could not help but stare incredulously out of the lift and wonder if they were tap shoes he was wearing.

The newspaper photographer arranged his first ever exhibition of photography, comprising mostly of private pieces he had never allowed the public to see before for fear they would be declared ugly and uninspired. It was a success. The city's nudist society finally came out of their very comfortable but concealed closet and registered themselves as an organisation in the city telephone book. Her mother fulfilled a life-long dream and sold her old car, using the money to buy a classic motorbike, complete with red leather jacket. An airport worker ripped off all his clothes one afternoon and stomped violently in an ornamental pond in front of the departures entrance, shouting: 'It's all for you, Renata!'

About a month after the incident, when most of the office jokes had been worn out and thrown away, Joel came up to her desk at the end of the shift. He had not spoken to her since the brief conversation in the lift, and had to all intents and purposes crawled back into his strange little shell.

He had a local poetry magazine in his hands, flicked through to a page and handed it to her without saying a word. A little confused, Renata took the opened magazine and quickly glanced over the poems, not really sure what she was supposed to be looking at. Then the name at the top of the page caught her eye. Joel Garcia. She looked back up at him, considering him in a new light. "I didn't realise you were a poet."

"I'm not really; it's just something I do in quiet moments here. I'd never dared send anything in, but after what you did, I thought I should take a chance and do it."

"Well, that's great, Joel," she smiled warmly, handing him back the magazine. "I really hope you keep this up now that you've started."

"Oh no, keep it," he gestured towards the magazine. "I wanted to say thanks; you inspired me to do this. I admire you."

"Yeah, you said that last time we spoke, in the lift," she said, closing the magazine and smoothing down the cover. "Remember? You said you admired what I did."

"That's not what I meant," he started awkwardly. "Although I do admire your courage, what you did. But I meant that I've always admired you. I never understood why your boyfriend left you." He stopped talking abruptly, wavered indecisively in front of her for a moment before nodding. "Better go shut down my computer and head off home."

Renata was silent. Stalled by the direct comment. Everyone in the office had known about her boyfriend of course, he knew Cindy, and when he had left Renata, Cindy had been sure to let everyone know, on a supposedly sympathetic pretext. The poor girl who was 'a little bit fat'. Renata watched as Joel moved uncomfortably through the room to his computer. God, he was shy. And that was what he had been doing so secretively over there in the corner, pouring his heart out into words.

Opening the magazine again, she flicked through to the page filled with his work. The longest piece was entitled 'My Muse' and described a beauty, an amazing creature that inspired him. Renata's eyes widened and she felt a warm pink touch her cheeks. She was not vain and did not have an over-inflated opinion of herself, but it was so embarrassingly obvious that she was the object of the poem.

She raised her head, snapping the magazine shut as Joel shrugged his jacket on. Dark green. The colour suited him very well. "Hey, Joel," she called over to him, surprised by her boldness, but pushed on by the thought that she might regret it if she did not take the chance. "It's too hot for cooking. I can't be bothered, so I was going to go down to that Italian café on the corner, you know the one? Do you want to join me?"

Joel smiled. "Sure."

Part Four
Come and Give Yourself a Hand

Antonio Jerez, Wendy Jerez and Elena Montello grew up in the same stone-shack village in the mountains. It was a long way from Jimanac, even further than the crow flew, what with the rough narrow mountain dirt tracks that only rickety carts pulled by donkeys had the endurance to make it up. Antonio and Wendy were the last of the Jerez children, Wendy being a bit of a disappointment for the family with her terrible eyesight. She was so short sighted that it simply wouldn't do to let her go wandering on her own for fear that she would unwittingly stroll off a cliff. So the child was forced to stay at home most of the time, getting under her mother's already overburdened feet and driving the woman to distraction. Her mother swore there would be no more children, fearful of what disabilities would come next, and her father was forced to sleep out in the disused pig shed for the next fifteen years.

Wendy and Elena were best friends. They attended the little school set precariously on a precipice overlooking the valley. Wendy had no real academic talent, but the teacher saw a spark of wisdom in Elena. Yet the girl could not be persuaded to leave her family and move down to the lowlands to get a real education. Her teacher thought it was because she was too afraid to leave her family, to say goodbye to the mountains, but in truth she was too devoted to Wendy. Wendy was the greatest friend any little girl could have, and her dog-like loyalty, a side affect of constantly needing a guide, meant that Elena was never alone at the side of the playground.

Of course Wendy went through several pairs of glasses during those years but they never helped. The optician only came up to the village once a year, and it took over two months for the prescription glasses to arrive, by which time Wendy's eyesight had already worsened. She had brief moments of burning clarity whilst she sat with strange spectacles on her face, then she was plunged back into blurred vagueness. The dogs were too wild there to be reliable guide dogs, so Wendy had to take people's help instead.

The one real talent Wendy possessed was lace making. It was almost a contradiction in terms, for her eyes were poor and she could not see the intricate patterns she made. She could feel them however, and had incredibly sensitive fingers. When she got the chance to drop the more serious subjects she left the academic school and went to the home economics class. It was essentially a glorified meeting for hopeless young girls who would one day be wives in the mountain community. They were taught by an old woman with no teeth. Wendy was the first to sign up. Elena's name was second.

The girls learned about cookery, sewing, cleaning and child care, and life stagnated up in the mountains. Their peers from the school read their scruffy textbooks – rejects from the lowlands – and several eventually left, hoping to find themselves and their fortune somewhere in the wider world. Elena and Wendy would sit outside the Jerez house making lace tablecloths whilst watching children, now teenagers, head off down the mountain track to the modernised world. They would listen to the sound of the panpipes, gaze up and the clear blue sky baked in dry heat, and tell themselves that they had everything a person could ever want right here. The Jerezs and the Montellos knew what was right in life.

One day Antonio, Wendy's elder brother, declared that he had had enough of the village, and was going to Jimanac to become an engineer. His father, chasing chickens out of his bedroom, laughed at the declaration, and no one took him seriously until one morning he was gone. Wendy was devastated, for she idolised her brother. She barely spoke a word that first month, until a letter from Antonio, dated two weeks past, arrived in the village. The next two years saw a succession of letters to and from the village, detailing Antonio's life and adjustment to the modernised rush of Jimanac. It was so foreign to what he had grown up with that it may as well have been another planet. However, Jerez people were strong and adaptable, and Antonio learned the ways of the city, accounting every eccentricity to his younger sister. He got a job packing boxes, rented a room and took his national exams. After that he upgraded to a job in an office, working with strange things called computers, and enrolled on a night school university course in engineering. After his first year in Jimanac he was able to move into his first small apartment – which, according to Antonio, was more than adequate for a whole family and three goats. Here in Jimanac everyone seemed to need a lot of personal space, which was why it was so big in comparison to the village, he supposed. It was probably also why there were a lot of lonely and isolated people.

The following year the girls turned eighteen and it was time for marriage. Wendy retreated into the house and refused to come out, begging whoever she could to read through her brother's letters to her. Several boys hung around Elena - people said she would make a good wife - but Elena told them all no. She did not want to leave Wendy alone. So the two girls hid in the shadows, going through Antonio's old letters and listening to their mothers complaining in the kitchen. They could not sit and hide forever.

One morning Wendy came up with the solution. They would move to Jimanac. They packed their few possessions, said goodbye to their families, who in turn were certain this move would come to no good, and took the next donkey cart down to the lowlands.

As it transpired, Wendy and Antonio had been secretly planning this great move for some time. Antonio had found a small apartment for the girls. He had even paid the first month's rent, although he could do no more than that and told them they would have to get work to pay their own way. By that he meant that Elena would have to get a job, because Wendy's eyesight did not permit her to do very much.

For the first week Elena did not dare leave the flat. She was overwhelmed and terrified by the enormity of Jimanac, the constant sounds and noise, the strange smells and the thickness of the air. She was surrounded and consumed by a constant rush. The realness of the cars was frightening, for she had never experienced such things apart from in picture books. Gradually she moved closer to the window, and watched the world from a safe distance, learning from observation the ways of Jimanac.

Elena eventually got a job in a small café as a waitress. Wendy stayed at home and listened to the radio whilst doing a little lace work. They were all waiting for the day Elena would be paid. When the money came in, the girls did two things. They paid the rent and Wendy went to the opticians with a fist full of money. Elena went out later in the week and bought a second hand television, the same day as Wendy got her glasses and saw the world clearly for the first time. Had Elena known what unfortunate events the two would have brought, she would have left the television in the shop and refused Wendy money for the eye test, but hindsight was not something she was gifted with.

Wendy was a little motion sick at first by the way everything loomed up at her in crystal clear clarity. She sat on the sofa for a week to steady herself, and abandoned all the radio programmes she had followed, turning instead to the television. She was hypnotised by the miracle, the tiny men and women that performed for her on screen. She watched everything: the films, the soap operas, the news, the fashion shows, the chat shows, the documentaries. Mesmerised by the beautiful people and their fascinating lives, she knew that was what she wanted, not to just sit in the flat like a housewife all day every day. Yet there was one thing that she had noticed, amongst everything she had gleaned from the land of television – beautiful people did not wear glasses. Wendy went out into the hall and stared at herself in the mirror. Her plain face, with bottle-lens glasses and dark eyebrows that met in the middle of her face in a most unpleasing way, would never be accepted into the fast, glamorous life.

The following weeks past by quickly. Wendy disappeared into her room and worked industriously on her lace tablecloths, which sold for high prices in Jimanac. Authentic mountain lace was something quaint and ethnic that the rich and the tourists liked to take home. She also took to pilfering money from the grocery jar, hiding the notes in one of her old shoes. Elena, against her conscience and her wishes, found herself starting to resent Wendy. She worked long hours, yet she never had any money for herself, she thought as she stood outside a shop window contemplating a red dress she simply couldn't afford. She went out on her first date that evening with a boy from the café. It ended disastrously. She had been looking forward to it; he was so friendly and modern, with so much to talk about. But whenever he asked her about herself, she always found herself talking about Wendy. No one wanted to hear about Wendy, the plain little blind girl who sat making lace tablecloths in her room. The boy eventually gave up, telling Elena she was boring. He walked out, leaving her with the bill.

Elena was in tears. She had worked a ten-hour shift, followed by a date that had destroyed what little self-confidence and self-identity she had thought she had. She was boring. That was the verdict. Boring and poor. She arrived home, her face streaked with tears, to find Wendy sat on the sofa with a large pair of dark sunglasses on, despite the fact that she was in a darkened room. She didn't have the energy to take on anyone else's problems, so she did not ask and went straight to bed.

She did not see Wendy the following day. Wendy did not leave her room. The day after Elena was not working. She got up to a kitchen table full of cosmetics that she could not afford. Wendy's glasses were lying on the table beside a bottle of face cream, and Wendy was stood in front of the hall mirror examining her scrawny body. She had no glasses on, yet she seemed to be able to see without any problem.

Elena gazed at her friend in confusion. It was a strange transformation. Wendy's eyebrows had been separated and plucked, and her face was covered in heavy make up. "How can you see?"

Wendy glanced up at her in an off-hand manner. "Oh, I got corrective eye surgery. Laser treatment."

Laser treatment? Elena had heard about this. "But that's really expensive."

"I've been saving up," Wendy shrugged it off absent-mindedly. "You know, I might get a little plastic surgery next," she added, tugging at her baggy top. "I am so shapeless."

"Plastic surgery?" Elena repeated, at a loss to think of what might have happened to her friend. "What's going on?"

"What's going on?" Wendy turned on her. "Life is going on. I have to get out of here; I can't sit in my room and make tablecloths. I've got to get out into the city, go to parties, and have fun. I'm going to get a job as a model or an actress. I've already found somewhere more central to live. It's just way too boring here."

"Boring?"

"Yes!"

Wendy was gone by the evening, her room bare apart from old cut off threads from her tablecloths. Elena sat in her empty flat with her empty soul. It was as if the homely, innocent sweet girl had left the flat just as she had left Elena's soul. Everything was boring here now; life and personality had deserted her and the flat.

Wendy's brother, Antonio, came to the flat when Elena told him that his sister had run off in wild passion. He did not seem too concerned; he said the city could do that kind of thing to people. Elena had stared at him in distress. What was she supposed to do? He had suggested that she tried to find herself; she could make it on her own. Wendy had only been holding her back from her true potential. Elena did not digest what he said; she just stared at the empty room and decided she needed a new roommate.

They let her put up a notice in the window at work, but there was no response the first week. Elena was near to giving up when Geoffrey visited the café. He was a short, plump man without a chin of any definition – merely a smooth outward curve from the tip where his chin ought to have begun out to his well-proportioned belly. His dark hair was swept back dramatically, and despite his small stature, he had the uncanny knack of being able to look down on everything and everyone. When Elena first saw him, he was complaining to one of her colleagues.

"Really, I don't know how you people dare sell this as food," he cried out as if auditioning for a part. "Look at this," he continued, picking up a piece of limp lettuce with his fork. "I've seen dishrags with more nutrition in them."

Elena stood at the side of the eating area and watched the one-sided conversation in morbid awe. Antonio had said that she needed to find herself and grow as a person. That she needed more confidence. This man had confidence, he knew his own mind and he wasn't afraid to show it. He wasn't pushed around by others, or shoved into insignificance. If only she could be more like him.

"Well, I'll get you a refund," the waiter muttered, glaring venomously at the stranger.

"Yes, and while you get on with that, I saw a notice in your window about a room. Do you know anything about it? If it's anything like your food, I don't know if I dare go see it."

"Actually, I'm renting out the room." Elena stepped boldly forward.

"You?" The man turned, eyeing her suspiciously.

"And it's clean and well priced. Nothing like the food here."

The man broke out into a wicked smile.

"What were you saying about the food?"

Elena jumped at the badly timed appearance of her boss's voice from behind. The man, whom she later learned was called Geoffrey, watched her intently; this was to be the moment upon all judgements on her personality were based. Did she have a spine? Did she really have opinions to be respected?

She turned and looked her boss in the eye. "Well, quite frankly, the food is revolting here. I know you want to keep the prices down, but that doesn't mean you have to give up on quality completely."

"Suddenly a food critic?" her boss spoke icily. "Well, I'll save a bit of money on your wages. You're fired."

Geoffrey's smile broadened even further. "I like you."

Geoffrey moved in that evening. He was an artist in every sense of the meaning, and had the temperament and lack of work to prove it. He wanted to be an opera singer, but was either deaf or deluded for he was just a big-bellied man with a loud voice. He could have sold vegetables on the street with enviable talent but the opera houses and theatres were not exactly queuing up to employ him. When he wasn't at auditions Geoffrey had four states of being: sleeping when he snored like a walrus; eating when he ate with his mouth open; practising when he warbled whilst strutting from room to room, and finally complaining, back stabbing and general vocal malice when he verbally tore everything and everyone to shreds. He had nothing nice or praiseworthy to say about anyone but himself.

At first Elena thought this say-what-you-think attitude to be admirable and the sign of a strong character. That had been her first impression in the café. But first impressions were not always to be depended upon. After a week of living with this over-inflated fool from the coast she realised he was just small-minded and lacking in character. She finally came to the end of her patience when he stuck his knives of criticism into a lace tablecloth that she had made several years ago. She stormed into his room, packed his bag for him and tossed him out of the flat. There was a limit to what any sane person could endure.

The following weeks were a period through which Elena wandered in a daze. She felt very alone, both in her flat and in her life. She got a job in an office typing up memos and letters and managed to pay the rent on her own. Yet it wasn't enough and she felt restless. She volunteered for a charity that cleaned the local streets of litter, as the dustmen only appeared there once a week, and she did the weekly shop for three old ladies living in her building: all to fill her time and to escape that gnawing sensation that something was missing.

Elena was introduced to herself one afternoon whilst returning home carrying a bag full of peppers. There was a little girl sat at the bottom of the steps up to Elena's building. The girl's face was streaked in tears. Her mouth was set at a permanent downward wail and the sound that came out was terrible. Everything about her was distraught, even the curl of her pigtails.

"Hey, what's happened?" Elena asked, setting her bag of peppers down.

The little girl stared up at her, coughing on her sobs as she tried to answer. "The boys knocked me down the steps."

"Did you hurt yourself?"

"My arm hurts," she stated. Merely uttering the words reminded her of her pain and the wailing started again.

Elena crouched down beside her and felt the little girl's arm. "I think it's broken," she said, feeling the surface of the bone under the flesh with her fingertips. "But don't worry, we're in the city and there are lots of hospitals and doctors here to take care of you."

"Excuse me, madam, what is wrong with your daughter?"

Elena glanced up to see a young man waiting politely behind her.

"She's not my daughter, and she needs to go to hospital now. It's her arm."

"Really?" The man dropped down to his knees in front of the girl. "I am a student doctor; I might be able to help."

The little girl's bottom lip started to tremble again as the man examined her arm, pinching at the flesh.

"Where is your mother?"

"She's working."

"It's broken," the student declared, satisfied with his diagnosis. He sat back on his heels, the look of contentment on his face. He was making progress, finally feeling like a real doctor. This was just the kind of confidence boost he had been looking for today.

The little girl pointed innocently at Elena. "She already said that."

Elena smiled weakly at the sight of the man's falling smile. "We should get her to hospital," she pointed out, jumping up onto her feet as she saw a taxi turn into their street.

Three hours later the girl's arm was being fixed as best it could, her mother had been located and was currently on the bus to the hospital, and Elena's sense of responsibility had been passed over to the hospital staff until the mother arrived. Waving goodbye to the little girl, Elena left the ward and made her way to the exit. As she approached the revolving doors she wondered to herself if her bag of peppers would still be waiting for her on the steps to her home when she got back.

"Wait up!"

The young student doctor appeared from the crowds of staff, the ill and decrepit, the repaired and the new-born who stalked the corridors of such places. He waved at Elena and hurried up to her as she waited patiently by the exit.

"It was very good, how you took care of that girl," he praised her as they walked out together into the evening sunshine. "And that you guessed her arm was broken. Maybe you should study to work with medicine."

Elena idly mused over the suggestion. She had always liked working with people, being with people, helping people, putting other people first, serving people... now that she considered it, her life was a long list of actions that did not revolve around herself. Perhaps there was something in what he said.

"Just think," he continued, talking as if they were old friends. "If you study to be a nurse, we might end up working together. We could study together..."

It would be nice to have someone else to be with, Elena thought to herself. Stop there, she scolded her mind. What she needed to do was start living through herself, not other people. Not that there was anything wrong with being a nurse, but it wasn't for her. Elena looked the student in the eye as they came to a road crossing. "I think I will take your advice."

His eyes brightened hungrily. "You're going to train to be a nurse?"

"No." Elena was quite certain on that point. "I'm going to be a doctor." A great doctor, she added, although silently for she did not want to hurt his feelings more than she already seemingly had. Maybe one day he would have the honour of working with her. Who knew what the future might bring?

Part Five
Student Theatrics

Alessandro and Mario had just stapled the poster to the entrance wall when the rock programme they were listening to was interrupted. Alessandro lowered the staple gun he had used to illegally attach the concert poster for his band to the entrance hall to this particular block of flats and gazed across at Mario's portable radio. Mario was rolling up the remaining posters as the news reporter's voice crackled through the evening air.

"We apologise for interrupting the current programme, but just a few minutes ago two gunshots were fired at the Golden Theatre during a performance of *Madame Butterfly*. We are outside the building now, which has been cordoned off by the police, and there is chaos here. No one is really sure what has happened, although it has just been confirmed that the Mayor of Jimanac has been shot…"

Mario dropped the posters and looked over at Alessandro. "Jesus, an assassination," he gasped. "I don't think such a thing has happened in Jimanac for over a hundred years."

"I wouldn't be so sure of that," Alessandro muttered grimly, wishing Mario would save the shocked-public commentary for later so that he could listen to the report.

"Mayor Alberto Hernando reached local headlines and number one place for heated discussion at the start of the year with his controversial suggestions..."

"A political assassination!" Mario burst out excitedly.

"...met with angry opposition..."

"We'll be on the national news, you know."

"...protesters marched to the town hall last week with a petition..."

"We should go to the theatre," Mario declared, picking up the roll of posters and shaking it excitedly in the air. "It isn't far from here. Maybe we'll get on television."

"Will you shut up!" Alessandro growled. His anger was in vain, for the reporter apologised once again for her interruption, and the radio returned to scheduled programming. The heavy monotonous beat of drumming vibrated out from the tinny portable radio. "Never mind," he sighed, leaning back against the poster he had just put up.

"All right, you're curious," Mario said, taking the staple gun from his friend and slinging it in his rucksack out of which the radio hung. It was very hard, if not impossible to offend Mario. "Let's get over to the theatre."

"No, you go." Alessandro's concentration was already wandering. Mario, back turned to the main entrance, was oblivious of the arrival of a pale young woman who was just now ascending the steps to the door in a most careful and graceful manner. She was attired in a dark-blue velvet ball gown - yards of skirt that required picking up whenever she wished to move. Her shawl, black and intricately crocheted, hung from her arms, her bare shoulders exposed to the night. Her long black hair was loosely tied back off her face but left to unfurl lazily down the centre of her back. It looked as though she had a hundred tiny pearls threaded through her hair, little beads that glowed like raindrops under the poor entrance lighting. She was keeping her eyes carefully unfocused on anything, but as she passed by her jeans-clad peers, she met Alessandro's eye for a brief moment.

"Your loss," Mario shrugged. "I'll see you tomorrow for practice."

The lift chimed as the carriage reached ground floor and the doors pulled open. Alessandro turned as the woman stepped into the lift, shifting around to face the entrance hall. She reached out slowly, regally, to press for a floor.

"Wait!" Alessandro ran for the lift, catching the doors as they moved to close. Pushing them back open, he scrambled into the carriage with the stranger. Smiling sheepishly at her – unnecessarily because she was looking intently at the number panel – Alessandro faced the front as the doors closed and they were confined together upwards.

He could not help but stare. There was something about her demeanour, her poise that was to be admired. It was as if she was controlling a great storm beneath, desperate to sink down and slouch in exhaustion, burst out into laughter or tears, scream, run away or simply stop bowing down to the gracefulness she was encased in. Her face masked all emotion, neither a crease nor a thought was betrayed in that calm stare.

"That's a very glamorous dress you've got on," he initiated conversation, cringing at the poor choice of words.

The girl slowly turned her head to consider him, but said nothing.

"An opera dress. Were you at the Golden Theatre tonight?" he blurted out eagerly. "It was just on the radio. There was gunfire. The mayor was shot." He lowered his eyes, feeling slightly ashamed that he was bothering her with these questions. He sounded naïve and immature. Besides which, the police would not have allowed anyone to leave the scene yet. All eyewitness accounts would be needed.

"I was there."

He looked up sharply, surprised by her words. She had not seemed willing to talk. Even now she seemed uncommunicative, staring back at the lift panel.

"You saw it?"

She nodded, a very slight movement of the head that could almost be missed. "He was looking straight at me when he was shot."

Alessandro was about to pursue her with more questions when the lift juddered and stopped prior to its destination. Unbalanced they both tumbled to the side of the wall, Alessandro righting himself first and stepping over to the buttons to try and restart the lift. The girl remained against the wall, her fingers stretched out across the grimy surface as if she simply did not have the energy to push herself back up.

"It's an old building," she told him as he pummelled at the control panel. "They should have replaced the lift years ago." She paused, closing her eyes for a moment as if a thought had just occurred to her. "I can't..." she bit her tongue mid sentence as Alessandro turned to look at her. "I have to get out of here." She reworded her original, unfinished statement.

"Maybe if I get the doors open we can clamber through," Alessandro suggested. "Although it's not very safe. If the lift carriage started moving again..."

"I have to get out of here," she reiterated.

Alessandro was the drummer in his band – something he did when he was not involved with his studies at the university – and he had strong arms. The lift doors were puckered and uneven and it was easy to get a grip on the two panels. With a little effort and straining, the doors began to pull apart.

The next floor was two feet higher than the floor of the lift. Alessandro pushed the doors wide open and scrambled out, feeling very much the hero. Taking an old fire extinguisher from the hallway, he propped open the doors high up, then turned back to the lift. The girl was so pale she looked like a ghost. He offered his hand. "You should get out quickly. In case the lift moves."

The girl held out her hand and Alessandro pulled her free of the lift. She felt so weak in his fingers. As she crawled out into the corridor, one of the doors along to their right opened and a woman stepped out. Leaving the door wide open, she leaned back into the flat to wave at someone. Alessandro looked up, having removed the fire extinguisher from the lift, as he heard the sound of a television from within.

"...the mayor was dead on arrival to the hospital. He died from a single shot to the back of the head. Investigators now have the..."

The door to the flat slammed shut and the woman started to walk towards him. She raised an eyebrow, looking from the lift to the fire extinguisher to Alessandro. "The lift is out of order, again?"

He nodded meekly.

Grumbling to herself, the woman pushed the stairwell door open with her shoulder and started her walk down seven flights of stairs.

It was a dramatic night. It had barely been five minutes since he and Mario had been down on the ground floor listening to the radio. The news flash had interrupted their favourite rock programme to inform them that two shots had been fired in the theatre. Now it transpired that the mayor had died from a single shot to the head. Two to one. Alessandro pursed his lips. Where had the missing bullet gone?

"You know, they said earlier that there were two shots." He turned around to speak to the girl just as she slipped through the door to the stairwell. Pushing open the door with a single hand, he looked into the stairwell, surprised to see that she was already half way up to the next floor. Yet the thing that surprised him the most, as he ought to have realised something was wrong by now, was the thick wet trail of blood that marked out her course. "You took the second bullet."

She stopped and looked back at him, smiling weakly. "Actually it was the first."

A moment went by slowly, silently, and he merely stared at her. His mind stared to catch up with the passing of time. "We've got to get you to a hospital." He stared up the staircase after her.

She shook her head as he took her by the shoulders for support. "No. Just help me get onto the roof." She continued walked up to the next floor.

"You took the first bullet. Everyone heard two shots. People are going to be looking for you. The gunman missed the first time and took an innocent bystander." He sounded like a newspaper now.

She smiled wryly. "I'm neither a bystander nor innocent, and the gunman did not miss."

They had reached the top level of flats. Alessandro stared at her, horrified. "You mean that the mayor was not the target?"

"Oh, he was a target."

"But why shoot you?" He gazed at her in a mixture of awe and bewilderment. "Who are you?"

"I'm no one," the girl responded, struggling with the door to the roof. Something fell from her dress. They both looked down, horror entering their facial emotions for entirely different reasons as they saw the revolver lying there on the rough concrete step.

Alessandro stared in bewildered awe at her. "You shot Mayor Hernando?"

The girl turned away from him and tugged at the door. "Please, open the door," she begged, avoiding his eye. "I need fresh air."

"We have to get you to a hospital," he responded, sounding like the responsible parent he wished he'd had, but he opened the door for her anyway. A rush of cold night air jumped in and bit at their flesh. "Where were you shot?"

She ignored him and picked up her weapon as she stepped out onto the roof, her heeled shoes tapping against the rough roofing material.

He felt as though he was caught up in a dream. It was too fantastical to be true. He ought to have gone out and called the police, an ambulance, someone responsible, but Alessandro was hypnotised by this strange girl. He could not let be. He had to know. "Why did you shoot him?" He followed her out into the night. "You're a political activist, aren't you? It was because of his proposals, wasn't it? They would have been bad for Jimanac…"

She had walked quite a far way out on to the roof, lit up by a background of twinkling lights from the city. A breeze moved over the top of the building. She looked back over at him. She did not understand why he was so interested – they were strangers after all – or why he would not leave her alone, but she no longer had the energy to force him to go. So she stood and gazed imploringly at him, the wind rippling through her ball gown.

"I went there to kill him," she confessed. "I took the gun from my fiancé's cupboard and I went to the opera. In the intermission I stood up. I remember him standing there, staring straight at me."

Alessandro was not sure what to say. She seemed so sad about what had happened. It was hardly the behaviour of a political extremist. "Which wing are you involved in?"

"It had nothing to do with politics."

"But then… why kill him?"

"He had been bothering me for months. You understand?" She glanced up, searching his eyes for some kind of comprehension. She did not care to spell it out graphically. "When I was alone in the office. I was very frightened. He threatened me, told me if I told anyone, he would tell my fiancé lies. My fiancé works with him. He's Hernando's bodyguard; one of them. I tried to tell him, I tried to get his help, but he wouldn't believe me and I couldn't say too much. And Hernando is crazy; he's so paranoid. He has three bodyguards and he carries a gun. There's no easy way to make him stop." She paused. Alessandro noticed her hands were shaking. "So I went there to finish it. But Hernando saw me and acted first."

"He shot you? But then you have nothing to run from. It was self-defence. If he has been harassing you all these months..."

Alessandro broke off as the girl pulled back the safety from her revolver and brought it up to her head. "No!" he broke out, running across to her. "It was self defence. You don't need to do this." When he pulled the gun from her hands, he noticed she was crying. There was a pool of blood forming on the ground at the edge of her skirt. "We have to get you to a hospital." He told her, snapping open the gun carriage to shake the bullets from their chambers so that they might become harmless.

"When he saw me there with the gun. When he saw how Hernando acted, I could see that he realised it was all true."

Alessandro watched the bullets drop to the floor. Eight unused bullets. Eight empty chambers. The radio report had said that Hernando had been shot in the back of the head. The girl had said that he had been looking straight at her. "You didn't shoot him," he finally realised. "You're innocent, you haven't done anything wrong."

But if the girl had not murdered Hernando, then someone else must have.

"It was the bodyguard?"

"It was my fiancé."

She stared into Alessandro's eyes. "He can't get away with it. He will go to prison for the rest of his life. I just want to rest now. I just want to lie down." She dropped abruptly to the floor, her skirts spraying out across the dirty roof amongst the rain streaked smog and bird droppings.

Her eyes were still open and she was breathing lightly as Alessandro lowered to his knees beside her. "Look, don't fall asleep," he told her, shrugging off his jacket and throwing it over her torso. "I'm going to have to leave you for a moment, get help. I'll be back soon."

The girl lay still as she listened to Alessandro's footsteps running back to the stairwell. She then shifted position, rolling over onto her back to stare up at the stars. She could rest easy now, the nightmare was finished. The truth was out even though she would never be able to tell the tale and her fiancé would not wish to talk about it. The pieces of the story had been fitted back together. Perhaps now she could find a little peace, she thought to herself as she closed her eyes.

Part Six
The Way Things Are

The central district of Jimanac, where the river passes through, is lower than the rest of the city. The original settlers built the first houses here, houses long since demolished to make way for features of modern city life. In the bottom of this central basin where the sun became trapped, beside the gushing flow of the river, was the main park. Palm trees intermingled with other tropical shrubs and plants spread their waxy green leaves out wide, unintentionally providing shelter for pigeons and visitors in the midday sun. Butterflies drifted on the rising heat. The central avenue was gritted with a brown-pink gravel and lined with dark green wooden benches with black ornate metal legs – every bench dedicated to the memory of one outstanding citizen or another, a name and a vague memory but little else.

Elsa had been here for the past thirty years. She knew the history of every bench in that damn park, but she knew she would never see her own name on a gradually tarnishing plate nailed to the back rest. She had just turned fifty – although she looked more like sixty-five – and if one had not made some kind of success out of oneself by this age, then one was never going to get anywhere.

Thankfully for Elsa, she did not have over-realistic expectations of life. She had never wanted for a fat bank account, an amazing career, a great husband or even to have made a major impact on human society. She did not even particularly want to be remembered, although to be brutally honest, there was nothing about her that was worth remembering. That thought was void of self-pity and based on nothing more than reality and acceptance. Elsa had once dreamed of the little things: a home of her own, a good meal in the evening, a warm bed at night; but she had gone without these things for so long now that they were little more than abstract concepts.

Grumbling in the direction of a small group of pigeons that were daring to edge closer, she took off her grubby mittens – for the sun was high enough in the sky for her not to need her night wear – and picked up the half-eaten sandwich she had been overjoyed to find in one of the park bins that morning when she had woken up. It must be an exclusive sandwich, for it was wrapped in very fine white paper with delicate illustrations printed in dark green ink. It was still crisp, even after the damp night they had endured. She bit into it; thoughts of who had already bitten it – the mouths of rich and poor meeting – and why the sandwich was unfinished, irrelevant to her sensibilities. She savoured the feeling as the mayonnaise ran out from between the thick slices of bread, encircling her lips. This was a lucky find; it wasn't the kind of thing you found every day. Usually it was crusts and leftovers; the last few drops in a drink can. Once, about fifteen years ago, she and another had found a bottle of champagne, still half full, in one of the bins. That had been a good night.

Elsa was homeless. Elsa was a tramp. Elsa was a bag lady, with her old shopping cart parked defensively up beside the bench. She had lived in the great outdoors of Jimanac for the past thirty years, the past twenty in this particular park. It was only by the grace of the warm climate of Jimanac and her cunning mind, that she had survived this long, for most did not last so many years out on the streets.

She was a small, thin woman, with leathery, sun-worn skin, a wrinkled face and small black eyes. Her hair was knotted up in a bun, hair that she never washed and never brushed. When it grew so that the knot sagged, she could roll it up a bit higher. Over the years her hairy bundle grew, gradually layered like a tree. There were times when her head was covered with grease – not that she cared – but as Elsa knew, if you leave you hair long enough, it will clean itself. Her head was infested with fleas and lice on a regular basis, but she always had a bottle of powdered head lice remover in her trolley; one of the first things she stocked up on with money she got from the occasional begging; and she would regularly dust her head off as if she was a cake. She had a shabby, dark violet velveteen hat that she kept pinned on her head, almost to hide the extent of the state her head was in. She had some pride left after all, and she did not need passers by staring at her fleas in morbid fascination.

Finishing off the last crumbs, licking her fingers in satisfaction to the audience of disappointed pigeons, Elsa smoothed out the sandwich paper on her lap. It was very fine paper, there ought to be a use for such paper, and if nothing else, it would always serve as a reminder of that marvellous breakfast. Folding the paper neatly in half, she stretched across and set into one of the many plastic carrier bags that filled her trolley.

She froze as a creak groaned along the length of the bench. Cautiously, suspiciously, she slipped back into position, and without trying to make it too obvious, she examined the rest of the bench to see who had joined her. Her first presumption was that it must be another one of the homeless, for regular citizens never dared sit near her. There was always a risk that old Willie had crept up to try and steal some of her precious items; the old sod had taken two perfectly good green glass bottles from her trolley once. She would not let that happen again.

Elsa was surprised to discover that she was mistaken in her presumptions. The man sat on the bench was refined, well dressed, and to put it frankly, you could smell the money on him. He was the grey man, with silver grey hair, a grey wrinkle-free suit and dark grey shoes, freshly polished. He carried a dignified air, and a faraway look. He was probably a great businessman, making international deals, flying around the world, making and breaking the future of thousands upon thousands of workers. It was a life barely imaginable for Elsa; she had never even been out of the city limits of Jimanac.

The man opened his mouth, shifted his gaze as if he were about to say something, but the words hesitated and he just sighed. Elsa shuffled awkwardly, something that essentially never happened these days, as she was long past caring what others thought. She was the one who made happy couples and strolling philosophers uncomfortable with her presence. Elsa looked down at her dirty mittens; suddenly ashamed of them, she stuffed them into her coat pocket.

"Tell me," the man spoke without prompting. He still stared away into the distance, but there was no doubt that he was talking to Elsa. Besides, there was no one else in the park at this time of the morning. "If you had a million, what would you do with it?"

Elsa raised her eyebrows, almost as if she was insulted. "What makes you think I don't have a million?"

He smiled wryly at this comment, and for the first time shifted in position and looked her straight in the eye. "How long have you been living here?"

"This park? Maybe twenty years now. I can't complain."

"It's a very fine park," the man agreed. He looked a little concerned, to think that this woman had lived here for twenty years. "But have you never been able to get yourself a home? A roof over your head?"

"And how do you propose I do that?" she sniffed at the very suggestion. These rich, happy people had no idea how the other half live. "I have no address so I can't get a job. I have no job so I can't afford rent. It's the way things are."

"The system, it's a terrible thing," he agreed. "So what would *you* do with a million?"

"I would buy a house and move in of course!" Elsa responded sharply. It was such a stupid question. "So what would you do with a million?"

"Oh, I have several millions," the stranger replied in an off-hand manner. "Or at least I do at the moment. My wife is filing for divorce. She will take as much as she can get. She is very greedy. I think she only married me for my money…"

Elsa felt uncomfortable in this sudden splurge of intimacy. She did not know him, why was he opening his soul to her? She looked down at her shoes. They did not match, and there was a hole in the toe of one of them. She would have to try and find at least one new shoe, in the bins or left somewhere.

"And she will get millions. She doesn't even need it. I know already what she will do with the money, fritter it away. She is a spoiled greedy child. And it is so unjust, because there are people like you who could make much better use of a million…" he drifted off and looked across at Elsa as if the light of inspiration, the answer to all his woes, had finally come to him.

"What is your name?"

"Elsa."

"But your full name?"

"You mean my second name?" Elsa paused thoughtfully, trying to remember her old ties to the civilised world. "Abun. My name is Elsa Abun."

"Elsa Abun," the man repeated as he took an elongated notebook from his jacket pocket. This was followed by an expensive looking pen. He opened his pad and began writing. He did not have many notes to make, and soon his proud work was completed. Satisfied that he had finally done something right, he tore off the page and handed it to Elsa.

"This is for you, Elsa Abun," he spoke as he stood up, pocketing the pen and the notebook. "May it bring you happiness and shelter."

Elsa was deaf to him, staring in pure shock at what she had just been given. It was a cheque for a million. Was this the thing they called Karma? She would be thrust from one extreme to another to make an even balance of her life. In the breath of a second, she, Elsa Abun, bag lady and despised homeless person, had become a millionaire.

The obvious place for any discerning wealthy person to be seen was the National Bank – just the bank that had so kindly provided her benefactor with the chequebook necessary for supplying her wealth. Once the man had left – Elsa waiting as if any strong display of emotion would have been a sign of disrespect to him – she pulled the chock out from behind her trolley wheels and headed out of the park for the first time in months.

The like of it was unheard of, one of the homeless, one of the destitute, heading for the rich quarter, where all the law firms and exclusive banks were situated. Elsa was new money now, and with a sudden sense of quality, she wanted nothing but the best.

People stepped aside with a mixture of bewilderment and disgust as the old bag woman came trundling up the clean street, dragging a squeaking, rusting shopping trolley behind her. They would huddle in clusters at the side of the pavement, passing comment on the strange creature that dared to step into their blissful world. Some even shuddered, despite the warmth of the sun.

She soon reached the intended bank, gazing up at the glowing, immaculately clean sign as if it were a portent from the gods. Swinging the shopping trolley around, she parked it up outside the main entrance. The sudden jolt shifted the plastic bags enclosed within, and a strange smell erupted from somewhere within the masses of objects she had collected and forgotten about over the years. Elsa had very little sense of smell left, and already numbed by her own unique body odour, did not notice the distinctly unpleasant stink from her personal belongings. Trusting that the people in this area were too well off to want to steal an old woman's possessions, she walked confidently into the bank, clutching her cheque.

The counter staff smelt Elsa's entrance before they witnessed it, and all involuntarily leaned back from the clear plastic screen separating them from clients. It had been a quiet morning up until now, there was no queue, and Elsa would have her pick of the employees. Every single person working that shift prayed they would not be that unfortunate being.

The young woman who had only been with the bank a month; still full of company policy, idealised in company-client relations, and still far from the disillusionment that had hit many of her co-workers, wrinkled her nose and tried not to gag as Elsa approached her counter.

"Good morning," she chirped, immediately regretting such a deep intake of air. Elsa ignored the pleasantries and went directly to business. She was lost to social niceties, for out on the street there was no place for such meaningless gestures. If you stopped to say 'hello and how do you do?' you were more than likely going to loose your bench for the night and those few crisps you spied lying in a half-eaten packet.

"I've got a cheque." Elsa declared, pushing it under the screen to the girl. She was not sure quite what she ought to request, only that she wanted her money now.

"Well, what do you want to do with it?" the girl asked, gingerly accepting it. "Do you want to cash it?" She glanced down at the educated flair that had filled in the cheque. One million. This was a little more than she had presumed such a woman would have. Surely if she was so rich she could afford some reasonably new clothes and a little perfume.

"Perhaps not." Elsa responded. "That's too much cash to be carrying around."

"Quite right." The girl pushed her chair back from the counter slightly. "Well, we can deposit this into your account, and then you can just use your cash card to get money out whenever you need it. Do you have your account number?"

"I don't have an account."

"You don't have an account here?" The girl raised her eyebrows, wondering exactly what this woman was expecting.

"Don't have an account anywhere," Elsa stated truthfully. This was not going to be quite as easy as she had presumed. It was hard to know exactly what she ought to do. It had been so long since she had really been in civilised society that she really couldn't recall how the system worked. "I'd like an account here."

"And then you can deposit the cheque," the girl concluded for her. "Very well. I will need some form of identification to open an account."

Elsa narrowed her eyes. She should have known these people would try to play games with her. She had no identification. She had never travelled anywhere, she had never taken her drivers licence and she had certainly never opened a bank account before. How could she gain identification now, with no address and no purpose? Some days it was hard enough to remember who she was herself, never mind proving it to the rest of the world.

"I've changed my mind," she abruptly snapped, her mood swiftly souring. "I just want my money."

"I need identification," the girl reissued the request. "How am I supposed to know that you are..." she broke off, examining the piece of paper she had been given. "Elsa Abun?"

"Because I gave you the damn cheque!" Elsa threw back, her voice rising in volume.

The girl was uncertain how to proceed. It was doubtful that logic would win this argument. "That doesn't prove anything, madam," she replied politely. "If you think like that, then I could be Elsa Abun now. I am holding the cheque."

Fury lurched up in Elsa's eyes. "Give me my damn cheque!"

"Are we having problems here?"

The girl's shoulders sagged as the voice of her superior, a smug and highly patronising man from the south, appeared from behind her. He had been constantly omnipresent behind her during her first weeks here at the bank. He had been absent the past couple of days, and she had thought with a smile that management now deemed her capable to work on her own. Clearly it had just been a test she had somehow just failed.

She swung around on her chair to try and look him confidently in the eye. "This lady wants to pay in this cheque, but she will not give me any identification."

"Lady?" He raised a solitary eyebrow in a suggestive arch. "I somehow suspect that she does not own any identification. Not only that, but I would go further and suggest that this is not even her cheque."

Elsa was ready to fight for what was hers by this point, nails out and prepared to scratch. She would draw blood and she would poke out eyes if she was forced too. "You give me that back!" she screeched as the supervisor took the cheque from the girl. "You…"

"Guards!" shouted the supervisor.

Bank guards rushed across, heavy footsteps echoing on the cold, polished flooring slabs that covered the massive entrance hall. The supervisor smiled like a demonic cat as the two well-built men picked Elsa up by the arms and bodily escorted her from the building, her feet dangling above the ground. Elsa screamed and cursed, but to no avail. That was the last she ever saw of her fortune.

Having been thrown back on the street, Elsa was horrified to see someone emptying her trolley of all her plastic bags. Scrabbling up from the dust, she hurried across, waving her fists at him.

"What do you think you're doing?" she yelled as the man started to push the trolley away. She jumped in front of him as if daring a game of chicken, facing him down in the headlights of his single-tracked mind. "That's my trolley."

"No," the man retorted simply. "This trolley belongs to the supermarket where I am a manager. I am taking this back where it belongs." Pushing her out of the way as if she were a trifling insignificance, he started to wheel away the contraption.

"Since when did managers care about trolleys?" she demanded furiously.

As he hurried away with the trolley, he glanced back over his shoulder at her. "Where I work, we care."

Leaving the line that came from a bad advertisement as her final memory of him, he turned the corner up at the cross-junction and disappeared from sight. Elsa sighed deeply and looked down at her mouldering collection of plastic bags. Today had not been a good day. She wished she had never met the millionaire at all. Money only led to trouble and misery. She had heard it said many times and now she had experienced it for herself. That was the last time she would try to be rich.

"God damn it!" she cursed to no one in particular. There was no point trying in this world, you would never win at the game.

A dark green bag rustled, drawing her sharp little eyes away from the group as a whole. It moved again, as if something stuffed in the bottom was trying to get out. No matter, she couldn't possibly carry all these bags away with her, so that one could stay, perhaps as a little gift to the bank that had taken her fleeting moment of wealth away from her.

Selecting four bags from the heap of refuse that marked her life, she hobbled away from the bank with a sour look on her face.

That day was not a good one for Elsa. It had started so promisingly, yet she had been a fool to trust in any ideas of karma and the equalling out of luck. She had actually hoped that it would be possible, for she had suffered greatly during her life. Karma ought to have handed her a million in cash and a mansion in the hills. Karma had been lost somewhere, of that she was convinced.

Tramps are not as senile as they may appear to be to the passer by who hurries along and hopes they are not approached. The familiar faces had seen her leave the park, and immediately picked up on the fact that when she returned, she had lost her wheels. Her trolley was gone, as were the majority of her worldly goods. One of the few pleasures for people down in the gutter was revelling in other people's misfortunes.

She was mocked and ridiculed for the rest of the day. Elsa was just too angry to respond, and sat like a wind-worn statue on the park bench: her face taught and unresponsive, her eyes blazing with anger at the injustice of the world. Whatever she did, she was damned. There seemed little point other than to sit here and wait for the end. Daylight hours passed by and dusk sank upon them, blotting out colours and pulling shadows from their hiding places. A couple of tramps filled a metal wire rubbish bin with wood and newspapers, setting the contents alight. A beacon in the darkness, they stood around the hypnotic flames chattering and warming their dirty fingers, heating up various scraps of food they had gathered over the day. The world continued in the fashion it had always moved. Things were not meant to change.

Elsa's eyes flashed irritably as someone sat down beside her. She glanced across, shuddering to see it was old Cuth: a grey grizzly bear of a tramp with a flabby face, scruffy hair and a green woollen malformed hat permanently set upon his head regardless of the weather. There was a rumour going around the residents of the park that under the hat was a balding patch. Cuth was a man who was unnecessarily vain.

"Now, Elsa," he greeted her casually, spooning some cold baked beans from a can into his mouth. He paused, offering her some – an offer replied with disdain – before continuing. "I see you lost your trolley today. No one was as surprised as I was, because I know how fiercely you defend that heap of rusting metal. What happened?"

"You think I want to talk to you!" Elsa screeched, speaking for the first time since the drama at the bank.

"Probably not, but I am here anyway. You know, someone saw you talking to that rich man this morning. Said he gave you a piece of paper."

Elsa's eyes narrowed. They were like vultures, circling around and ducking down for scraps. They would be gravely disappointed this time.

"Then you leave the park, trolley and all. Disappear for hours, then return with only a few plastic bags. This is strange, indeed. What happened? Did he buy your trolley off you?"

She scowled. "You know full well he did not," she spoke indignantly. "If you must know, he gave me a cheque for a million and I went to the bank to claim my money. I should be in my own home by now! But they refused me my money, said I needed identification."

Old Cuth laughed, not a malicious laugh, but a sad, wry response to the way of the world.

"Then someone took my trolley saying it did not belong to me."

"Well, that much is true."

"They took my cheque. That had my name on it."

"For a moment you were a millionaire. This is the system. It is designed by the rich and the fortunate to sustain them in their perpetual state. And to keep the poor and the luckless down. For if we were all rich, there would be not enough wealth to go around. And if we were all well-off, to be well-off would have no meaning for we would have nothing to compare it against."

"It's not right," Elsa muttered.

"It's not right, but it is the way of the world," Cuth sighed. "You may wish the world to change, but it won't. You're just as well waiting for the snow here. You know it doesn't snow in Jimanac, we're too close to the equator."

Elsa waved her hand dismissively at the end. "So it is all for nothing."

"Perhaps so. But it is a waste of time to become angry over the system, over our bad luck. This is the way of the world and there is nothing we can do. We must accept our fate."

Elsa pursed her lips together and said no more. Cuth was renowned for being pessimistic in a dry, realistic way. Local hearsay had it told that he had once been a well-respected professor who had lost everything on an ill-informed bet on the horses. Everyone had his or her own way of dealing with personal tragedy.

Setting her mitten-warmed hands back on her lap, she noticed some white fluff on one of them. Raising her hand to blow the dirt away, she was surprised by its delicate form, witnessed for a moment before the thing disappeared, seemingly melting away and becoming one with her mitten. What was that?

Leaning back, she gazed up at the sky, where the dark backdrop was speckled with tiny dots of white fluff falling from unseen reaches. Gently, gracefully, they wound their way down air currents to settle on the ground, on fabric, on trees and grass, to become caught up in strands of hair. She looked across at her neighbour.

"Well I never," Cuth laughed as he looked around him. "It is actually snowing. Maybe we have waited long enough. Perhaps change is on the way now."

Elsa gazed across the park, the other tramps and bag women suddenly silent, captivated by the falling snow, the first Jimanac had seen in over a hundred years. She wondered what tomorrow might bring.

Part Seven
The Sad House of Cats

Anna-Maria was unpaid and unemployed, yet many took her to be a professional mourner. That was to say, she had the role down to an art of perfection. Her standards were those of a professional. She cut a sorrowful figure, a black vision with no obvious connection, and was probably there to bulk out the funeral procession. Yet as she never informed anyone of her services, indeed never considering her presence being of anyone's benefit apart from her own, she was not paid for the countless hours she spent in the graveyards and cemeteries. Sometimes beyond the call of duty, long after all the grieving relations and old friends had departed. In short, Anna-Maria was rather odd.

During waking hours she was usually sighted at one of Jimanac's graveyards. She never spoke and she was always alone. As the long years had passed, caretakers, gardeners and funeral directors had come to recognise her face and wonder exactly what it was that she did. Despite the curiosity and theorising over tea breaks, no one dared ever go up and talk to her; fearful that under that silent, still surface, there was a homicidal lunatic desperate to break out. After all, it was hardly normal behaviour to spend so much time in graveyards. Especially when you didn't know anyone there.

She was probably in her mid-thirties, a slender little thing always in high heels to get her height over five feet. She had dark hair that was cut in a savage, sharp and very exact line around her jaw line. It seemed as though she poured a jar of glue over her hair every day, for sections curved in this direction and that like wide crescent moons. She had large eyes that were always emphasised by heavy amounts of dark eye make-up that tended to run in the midday sun, giving her a very distressing look. She had a seemingly limitless collection of long black dresses and heavy Victorian jewellery. Back in the days when she had just started spending her days in the graveyards, a young man at the local art college had followed her about taking pictures. He had been utterly fascinated by her. It had become some sort of amusement and light relief for the graveyard caretakers, watching him follow her; her pretending not to notice. Until one day the young man stopped coming. He simply disappeared and was never seen again.

Some people thought she was a psychopath. Some pitied her; some feared her. Most were not aware that she existed, and even if they had known of her, they would not have cared.

Anna-Maria was far more complex that the gossip of undertakers' offices would suppose. She was essentially a misunderstood character. She spent so much time in graveyards because she was utterly miserable, and felt a close affinity with the dead. Besides, she was also quite keen on gothic art, fashions and nuances and felt the only way to follow this through to a pleasing end was to go with her interest through to mind-consuming obsession: wandering the tracks lined with gravestones, tombstones, crypts, memorials, stone angels, crying saints and the most famous of all dead inscriptions, R.I.P.

When people saw her she was like a living statue, her face void of emotion, her limbs moving stiffly as if she had just risen from her own mouldering coffin. When she was completely alone she would come to life, taking out small sketchbooks and pieces of charcoal from her pockets or voluminous sleeves of particular dresses, to sketch the gravestones, the lay of the land and the atmosphere of the day. Her studio at home contained a detailed record of all the graveyards of the city stretching back over the past decade. Not only that, but it all honesty, it was a stunning collection of artwork. If only someone was able to see it.

She lived in a small rickety house on a crumbling street up in the hills in the north district of the city. She owned the house outright, having inherited it from a spinster aunt who had been knocked down by a stream train one tragic summer day. The Railway Corporation had just bought a new train, and had arranged a celebratory free ride out to the coast for the people of Jimanac. The aunt, a spindly woman, had gone eagerly to the station with a bag of fresh fruit and a bundle of magazines. After a complimentary glass of champagne, she had tripped up on a running cat, fallen on the track and been crushed by the train as it reversed to be coupled up to the line of waiting carriages. A curse of cats had befallen the family since that day.

Anna-Maria arrived home that late afternoon, clutching desperately at her umbrella and trying to shelter from the lashing rain. Unlocking her front door, she staggered into the shelter of her dusty home, water dripping on the bare floorboards. At the foot of the staircase lay a dead cat – a grey siamese who had been quite healthy that morning. He had not even seen the week out in the house.

Scowling at the recent death, Anna-Maria tossed her sketchbooks onto the hall table and stalked across to her dead pet. She had always been rather fond of cats, and had always had a pet cat, ever since she had been a little girl. They had lived long lives until her aunt had died. Now they were forever dying. She stubbornly refused to give up, and as soon as one died, she was out to purchase her next pet, certain that one day the thing would see the year out.

Picking the cat, good old Nat, up by the tail, she carried the stiff little cadaver out to the back garden. Here was the great secret cemetery of Jimanac, a once luscious garden of olive groves and palm trees now filled with the tiny graves of over a hundred cats.

By nightfall Nat was safely tucked away in a hole in a ground. The shovel was propped up against the back door. Anna-Maria stood stock-still and surveyed her little empire. Things always died. Things always went wrong. Life was terrible.

After eating her evening meal and watering the plants – dark purple orchids and carnivorous pitcher plants were the only things that would grow in the house – she went out to visit the Magellan family down by Fountain Square. They were a prolific family with eight children all under the age of twelve; a fat, balding father; a tired mother; and a cat that spent wild nights out, paying the price several times a year with batches of kittens.

Rosa Magellan sat outside the front door on an upturned stone water trough that would have been used to water horses and goats a hundred years ago. She had a screaming baby in her arms, and had been requested to leave the house by her husband. She and the child were not allowed back in until the wailing had stopped.

She saw Anna-Maria coming down the street like a spectre and nodded to her, guessing why she had come. Anna-Maria approached the mother and child, and peered down at the infant's screaming face. The infant looked back at Anna-Maria and was immediately silent.

"Anna-Maria," Rosa greeted her, "Come now, cheer up. It is a beautiful evening."

Anna-Maria considered her glumly for a moment before responding. "My cat died."

"Oh."

"I don't suppose your Tigerlilly has kittens now, does she?"

"You came a day too late. We had to drown the latest litter; couldn't find no homes for them," Rosa sighed. "It's a real shame. I should have come up to you, but the children keep me so busy." She paused, looking up at Anna-Maria's face. She looked so sad. Surely she should be used to the death of cats by now. "When are you going to cheer up, Anna-Maria?"

"One of these days," she sighed, melancholy in her answer.

Rosa nodded to herself as she stood up. It was the usual response from Anna-Maria. She had been saying this for years now. "I might be able to help you, if you're looking for a cat." She ushered Anna-Maria into the house. "My man's sister moved to a flat where they're not allowed pets. She had a cat, a two year old, and it's been spade so there's no worry of kittens."

"You want me to take this cat?"

"Oh no." Rosa was quite certain on that point. "She's caught three mice already. I was wondering about Tigerlilly. We can't keep up with her kittens. Maybe she will calm down in a different neighbourhood. There are too many toms prowling around these streets."

Anna-Maria pursed her lips as she considered the offer. A kitten would have been best really, a young cat with lots of years ahead of it. She had had several kittens die, but she always felt they took the longest to give up and die. Tigerlilly had been around a few years, and not to put too fine a point on it, but she must be worn out. Not that Anna-Maria actually knew what was killing her cats off, but an exhausted cat did not seem to be the best candidate to stand up to unknown powers. However, a cat was a cat and she did not care for living alone. The cat would die soon, and Rosa would only complain, and then, what with the Magellans not having an overproductive cat, there would be fewer kittens to be had, but she supposed it was the best she could get at such short notice.

"All right," she finally agreed to the offer, although not overly enthusiastically.

"Good, she's locked in the kitchen at the moment, we'll go fetch her."

Rosa led the way into the cramped, chaotic little house. It was much smaller than Anna-Maria's house, she noted, and too full of furniture and people, but the Magellans did not seem to mind. The man, the lump known as Rosa's husband, was sat in front of the little black and white television, his stomach humped in front of him like a large sack of flour. He looked up as the two women walked past the doorway. Anna-Maria paused to regard him, thankful this kind of slavery had never been her destiny, and the man grinned condescendingly at her.

"Who died this time, Anna-Maria?"

She merely stared at him, deadpan, as if she had tried every expression there was to be worn, and nothing had suited her. Without a word, she walked away and headed towards the kitchen.

Tigerlilly, a stripped cat with large eyes and neat little paws, was currently curled up in a large bowl with the left over salad from the evening meal. Rosa set the baby in its cot and turned to the table, picking up the cat as if it was a large chicken for roasting. A strip of lettuce dangled from one of its claws.

"You have the bag?"

"Of course." The dark carpetbag was dumped ungraciously upon the table. She always took her new cats home in this. Tigerlilly was purring as Rosa set her into the rags that filled the bottom.

"I hope she doesn't get into mischief."

"Knowing my luck, she will procreate even more, my cats will stop dying and I will be over run with felines." Anna-Maria grumbled.

Rosa laughed. "You never know."

Considering she had lived at the Magellans' house all of her life, Tigerlilly accepted the move without even the slightest bewildered mew. When Anna-Maria arrived home and opened up the bag, the cat hopped out and scampered away as if this was well-chartered territory and she had been here many times before.

Anna-Maria wandered upstairs to her studio, flicking on the light and standing at a distance from the massive oil painting she was working on. It portrayed the ornate sculpture of the mausoleums and the tombs, of the age when the dead were truly honoured, back before this after thought slice-of-marble rage had come about. When it was finished she would probably just hang it in one of her empty rooms, as she had done with all of the pictures before.

Stepping out of her high heeled shoes – for she did not like to wear her good clothes in the studio, paint got everywhere – she walked, bare foot and small, across to the canvas. She took her black, full-length apron – stained with many streaks of black paint – and tied it around her waist. Pulling the small set of steps across, she hopped up and began adding highlights to a section higher up and out of reach.

The following morning, entering the kitchen for breakfast, Anna-Maria opened the cupboard as she always did, and pulled out the economy-sized packet of cereal. She screamed as she opened the box, dropping it in a shower of golden tasteless flakes as Tigerlilly smiled up at her from the confines of the opened crinkled plastic bag inside. As the box hit the floor, shaking like an orchestra of maracas, the cat sprung nimbly from the confines and moved fluidly out into the living room.

"Damn cat." Anna-Maria grumbled as she crouched down to brush up the disaster zone of breakfast cereal. "Damn mess."

"Starting the morning as we mean to go on?"

She looked up sharply at the cheery voice, to see the window cleaner peering in at her through the half-open kitchen door. Anna-Maria just scowled at him, and he soon scuttled away to wash the windows. Being a small woman who couldn't even reach the top of the ground floor windows, and a woman who owned a large house, she was a good client to have, but she was a grim, morbid little creature who was best avoided.

Anna-Maria looked back down at the pile of flakes she had scraped together. "Damn window cleaner," she swore to herself. Taking the dustpan and brush, she swiftly brushed up the mess. Yet as she was turning to throw the waste into the kitchen bin, she knocked the pan on the cupboard door, showering flakes out again at the foot of the kitchen sink. Rolling her eyes, she glowered at the ceiling. "Damn me."

Giving up on breakfast, she retreated to the living room to read a little gothic poetry or flick through a few Victorian horror prints. Tigerlilly was rolling around in one of the window sills, and upon hearing Anna-Maria's entrance, she sat bolt upright with a guilty look on her face. Dark purple petals stuck out of the corners of her mouth.

A quick glance at the orchids lining that particular window sill showed her the deflowered plants, now just rather bland green twigs coming up from the wide thick leaves at the base. Anna-Maria's eyes flashed and the cat took the hint as the window cleaner had, and crept away.

The pain and injury of her damaged plants was all the more brutal as today was her day for watering and general maintenance. She spent a good deal of time setting orchids back in their rightful places, picking up knocked flowers that now lay limply in the growing sunshine, brushing up bark chippings and soil that had been shaken from the various plant tubs. She was both horrified and mystified to see that someone had been around every one of her pitcher plants and put a frozen pea in each funnel; a pea that was now gently defrosting.

That damn cat. No wonder Rosa had offered it so willingly.

"Where are you?" Anna-Maria demanded hotly, slamming the watering can down on the coffee table. A questioning meow from the corridor gave away her current position. The cat was quite innocent of the growing fury in the living room.

Anna-Maria found the cat sitting calmly in the corridor, staring up at her with its big eyes. It made another little sound before scampering down to the back door, which was also open at a chink to let the house breath. The cat nosed the door open a little further, and holding its breath, squeezed its furry body through the space.

Anna-Maria hurried after the cat, not sure what she was going to do or what she was anticipating, but expecting an explanation, and stumbled out into her back garden.

Tigerlilly sat very still and gazed out across all the little mounds, some sunk down to ground level whose existence was only marked by a wooden cross or stake. So many cats that had died. Anna-Maria caught her complaints in the back of her throat. She said nothing instead, and padded outside to stand beside the cat and stare out onto the cemetery. Some of these sad little graves contained the offspring of Tigerlilly. She didn't suppose the cat was really aware of this, but a melancholy sank down onto the pair, as they looked out at the tragic back garden that morning.

Anna-Maria was particularly quiet and inactive in her own home after that. For the first day in several weeks, she did not go out, and did not even think of the funerals that she might be missing. She sat on her settee and stared at the wall and thought. Perhaps she ought not to have had cat after cat. She had always known they would die soon after moving into this house. Many of whom had been Tigerlilly's children. What was better really, drowning or suffocating in this place? Or was there really any difference?

There was a sound of something falling to the floor out in the entrance. Anna-Maria glanced up to see Tigerlilly come charging in, chasing a ball of rubber bands that she must have knocked off the hall table. She really was such a playful cat, considering the age she was.

The cat scurried after the ball as if it were a real mouse, watching with complete focus. As the ball rolled to a stop, the cat rolled playfully onto its side, before pawing at the little ball. One of her claws got stuck between two rubber bands, and she had to shake it off. Pausing for a moment, the cat looked up at Anna-Maria, mewed, then ran off into the kitchen.

When she went into the kitchen later for lunch someone had left out a cup of frozen peas. The cat – presumably it was Tigerlilly, for she could think of no one else who would do such a thing – had eaten all the flowers off the orchids in the kitchen windowsill, and in place had hung small red chilli peppers.

Anna-Maria was completely baffled. There was no logic to any of it. Or had things in Jimanac always been this way, and she had never noticed because she was always at the graveyards? No, that was too ridiculous. It was all quite mad. And for the first time in years, she broke out into a smile.

Things changed in that street after that day. A local painter and decorator was hired, and the outside painting was attended to. The exterior walls lost their shabby colour and took on a friendly glowing red. Every evening Anna-Maria could be seen sat out on her veranda enjoying a cool drink and sketching whatever it was that she happened to see at that moment. Tigerlilly lost her wild ways, and stayed at home on the evenings, stalking up and down the veranda fencing, chasing butterflies and mewing at the sunset. For a pair of lunatics, it really was quite serene.

Part Eight
The Peace That Comes With a Pie

Customers picking out fresh tropical produce from the street boxes at the green grocers paused as someone called out in a warbled voice: "Keep in place, people. Coming through." Confused at first, then slightly irritated and condescending as they saw who had spoken, they kept their places, for there was plenty of room on the pavement. There had to be something mentally wrong with the woman bustling down the street; how much room did she actually think she needed to get past?

Penelope, a woman laden down with plastic bags full of potted ferns, glowered back at the shoppers with equal annoyance as she hurried along. The air was hot and stuffy. Her brain felt as though it had been cramped into a vice that was gently, but steadily crushing the soft tissue of her mind. Her concentration on external measurements was off and she did not want to bump into anyone by accident and damage the plants she had just bought. The width of the pavement narrowed and burst wide open constantly in front of her. She counted her footsteps with blinks of the eye, eager to get home.

She soon reached her building, and with a gasp as if breaking free from the swirl of a watery grave, she staggered into the shade and flung herself into the lift. As the doors closed, she caught sight of herself in the mirror. The mirror shuddered as if wavering in the heat, and her reflection winked back as if it knew something she did not. Penelope groaned and closed her eyes. No more peyote. That cactus was no good for her.

Penelope lived on the top floor of an old apartment building constructed in the fifties. The flat itself was nothing to boast to mama milking the goats back in the pueblo, but the interior had never received much of Penelope's attention. The reason they, the royal we being her and her since departed – departed on a train to a different town and woman – husband, had taken the flat was because Penelope had refused to take anything else. She had wanted the flat for the roof space that came with the lease. Being the top flat, they had an area of thirty squared metres on the roof to do with as they pleased; or as it had turned out, as Penelope had pleased.

What had once been a blank, dull, infertile roof was now her garden of paradise. She had trees everywhere offering patches of shade from the hot Jimanac sun; large colourful clay pots of fruit bushes, plants and cacti; a stone garden ornament of a skipping dwarf – not your fishing fat fellow of most gardens, but a slender thing of original folk tales – and even a fountain with a small artificial pond, that was cast in Moorish style that she had seen on a holiday to southern Spain several years ago.

Bags of ferns now stood just by the door where they were going to be planted. Penelope went back indoors for a gardening trowel and a bag of compost. Crouched down beside the three tiered pot creation, she took the ferns out from the bags and arranged them in the large, glazed plant tub she had bought the week before.

Satisfied with her work, she lent back to admire it, before casting a proud gaze across her garden. Her survey stopped at the stone ornament of the dwarf. His nose seemed to have grown. Scrambling up to her feet, she hurried over to the dwarf, and wiped at his nose. The extra growth proved to be bird shit: a black and purple bubbled blob of crap dried solid in the heat. Her eyes narrowed and she looked to the door to her flat. Above the door, on the roof, sat a pigeon that stared back at her with casual indifference.

"What have you been doing now?" Penelope hissed. Her mind reeled at the possibilities, before she thought of her current project. The seedlings. A quick run past the fig tree took her to the nursery, where her once green and healthy seedlings were now ripped and pulled out, half eaten and trampled on.

"No, my supply!" she wailed, throwing her head back and crying like a banshee.

"Penelope, what's happened?"

She stopped wailing and looked to the open door, just as Danny, a friend from work, stepped out into the garden. She eyed him suspiciously, the woe of her destroyed seedlings abruptly forgotten. "How did you get in?"

"You forgot to lock your door. Again," he sighed, walking over to her. "I don't think you've had the door locked in the past two months. I know you live in a good neighbourhood, but it's not that good. Seriously, you have got to start looking after yourself better."

"Yeah, yeah, yeah," Penelope muttered, not really taking in what he was saying. She turned back to the seedlings, sifting through the damage with her fingers.

"So what's been happening? Someone destroyed your latest gardening project?" Danny crouched down beside her. "Jesus, Penelope, please tell me this isn't hash you're growing."

Penelope pouted stubbornly. "So what if it is?"

"You have got to start taking care of yourself. You've been so weird these past couple of months. You can't go on like this." He stared sadly at her. She was falling apart. Ever since her husband had left her, Penelope had been crumbling. It had started with the little things; turning up to work an hour late; drinking a little more coffee that usual, till it was chain coffee drinking, which meant she spent most of the working day going to the ladies' room. She forgot to lock her doors; she started to use drugs – although Penelope did not call them drugs or narcotics, instead referring to them as 'natural products' as if everyone ought to be on them. It was coming out in her appearance now. A year ago her hair had been full of beautiful natural brown curls. Curls that had needed regular attention, but Penelope had neglected them so long that they had degenerated to frizz. She had put a few butterfly clips in a few days ago to keep her hair under control but it looked like the butterflies were tying to take off, with feet full of wild, muddled hair.

"Look, I think you should take a couple of weeks off work," he started. "You need some time to get over this." To get over her husband. Sign the divorce papers and get it finished. The truly bizarre thing was that Penelope was better off without him, and she knew it. Danny wasn't sure if it was the sense of failure or the biting laugh of loneliness that was getting to her right now.

"What you really need to..." he broke off, realising she wasn't listening to a word he was saying. "What is it now?"

Penelope was staring back at the door with hate in her eyes. "That pigeon. That damn pigeon did this."

Danny twisted and caught sight of the pigeon before it fluttered up onto the roof and out of sight. He laughed lightly. "It will be company for you whilst you take a break. Besides, that pigeon did you a favour destroying these crops. Perhaps she is your conscience," he joked. "Pigeon Penny."

"No, don't you dare call it that."

"I'll see you in a week, Penelope," Danny called over his shoulder as he walked back into the flat to leave.

Penelope scowled at his retreating figure before standing up to her full height. Stepping to the edge of her garden, she lent against the art nouveux styled railings separating her from the long drop to the road far below, and gazed out across the vastness of Jimanac, the wind rippling through her long, baggy clothes. Maybe Danny was right; maybe she did need to take a break. If she took a week off work, she could really get to grips with the garden as well. She wanted to get some more flowers planted to increase the colour variation up here.

The following morning Penelope woke up to discover her bedroom window covered in bird droppings. Patches of sunlight broke into the room from between the splatter attack. Penelope threw the window open and lent aggressively out into the early Monday morning. "My plants didn't agree with you, I see?" she yelled at no one in particular. A passing seagull gave her an odd look before flapping hurriedly away. "Serves you right," Penelope muttered, stalking off to the kitchen.

She called her boss during breakfast to ask if she might take the week off. Her boss was surprisingly understanding, almost eager for her not to come in, and did not even want a reason. He made a comment about them not needing to buy another jar of coffee for this week. Penelope laughed along with him, but after she hung up, she wasn't sure if he had been joking.

After a breakfast of croissants and vibrantly orange marmalade, Penelope found herself in a pleasantly good mood. Ready to face whatever dilemmas the world may choose to throw at her, she flung her limp cloth handbag over her shoulder and left the flat to go shopping for food, actually remembering to lock the front door for the first time in weeks.

The walk to the supermarket became gradually distressing, and her paranoia was thrust up to emergency level. As she left the main entrance to her building, she saw Penny at the other side of the road pecking in last night's vomit with a couple of other pigeons. At the end of the road she was sat on top of a dustbin, staring intently at Penelope without blinking. Penelope hurried on past and pretended that she hadn't seen. She later saw her sat on top of a street sign, then scuttling along the street avoiding busy pedestrian feet, and even sat on a bus. She seemed to follow her everywhere, omnipresent like a bad smell.

Penelope burst into the sanctuary of the supermarket as if escaping a terrible blizzard. At least there would be no pigeons in here.

She was in the mood for cape gooseberries. They were ripe from the fields around Jimanac at this time of year. Basket in hand, she made her way to the fruit and vegetable section at the front of the shop. Engrossed in filling a plastic bag with the best selection of gooseberries. Something slammed into the windows at the front of the shop. Penelope cried out in alarm, involuntarily throwing her bag of small orange gooseberries into the air. It rained orange fruit around her as she looked to the source of terror. The culprit had since departed, but had left a calling card in the form of an imprint of a flying bird against the glass. It was perfectly pigeon-sized.

Leaving the supermarket with a modest sized bag of groceries, Penelope decided to take the short cut home back through the nearby park. It was a risky move, but she was eager to return home and find solace in her own private garden. As she neared the central lake - a small affair that gave home to a few ducks - she saw an old woman with a paper bag of corn feeding the pigeons. Penelope's eyes blazed, and she marched up to the woman, pigeons scattering at her feet. Staring down at the woman's old wrinkled face, she demanded furiously: "Are you insane? You shouldn't be encouraging them!"

The woman calmed contemplated the frizzy-haired creature before her, complete with a small orange fruit with dried papery leaves nestled in the rough of her hair like a freshly laid egg. She seriously doubted that anyone who walked around with pieces on fruit in their hair was in any position to tell her what to do. At the same time, she did not want to get into an argument with someone who chose to dress like that. Instead of replying, she merely shrugged and continued feeding the pigeons.

Frustrated by the world, Penelope marched away and hurried home.

The afternoon found her laid out on a blanket underneath her apricot tree. She had calmed down since the escapades of the morning, and had almost forgotten that pigeons had ever existed. Danny had been right about something, she had been a bit strange these past couple of months. Maybe she missed her estranged husband; although in all honesty she could not really say that she had ever been that fond of him. Perhaps it was the idea of him that she was missing.

Something wet slapped her on the forehead. She wiped at her forehead, horrified to see bird excrement smeared on the back of her hand as she lowered her fingers. A bird had just emptied its bowels in her face. It was the ultimate insult. Even before she saw her sitting in the apricot tree, she knew that Penny was responsible. The bird was perched in the foliage with that stupid look in its eyes. "You damn pigeon." she shrieked at the bird, scrambling up onto her feet. "When will you leave me alone? I'm going to get you!"

A desperate, tragically comical attempt at catching Penny ensued, ending with the pigeon flying off into the city, Penelope leaning over the railings throwing fistfuls of gravel in its retreating direction and hurling abusive words at the sun. Would she never have any peace?

She did not feel any better the following morning. As if nursing the mother of all hangovers, Penelope rolled herself out of bed and trudged to the door as she heard the post arrive: a birth of paper spewing out onto the doormat. She read through her bills and letters over breakfast. Her mother had sent her a letter – a regular monthly occurrence. The current issue was traditions and cooking; the wise woman had sent her daughter a selection of traditional recipes to remind her of her roots. Penelope's mother was convinced that city life destroyed the soul, and was anxious for her daughter. She was constantly thinking of ways either to get the country to her, or the girl to the country.

"Recipes, recipes," Penelope sighed, flicking through the hand-written cards. She stopped at the second to last one, reading the title a second time. A smile spread over her lips. Now this did sound interesting. Pigeon Pie.

Her plans for the morning revolved around her lemon tree. A crop of fresh lemons was ready for picking, and Penelope was trying to decide what would be best to do with them. She had a particular fondness for lemon sorbet but she didn't know if she had the energy for so much effort in the kitchen today.

Taking her basket from the cupboard, she wandered outside to her garden, and up to the lemon tree. Something was rustling back at the nursery. She narrowed her eyes, and turned in the direction of the noise. Because her garden was a rooftop garden, the usual garden visitors and pests never made it this high above their usual environment. In that respect she had an easier life than the ground level gardener. Yet there was always something that managed to get up here. The determination of some garden pests was almost admirable.

She smiled wickedly as she saw what it was that was tangled in the green netting that hung over her red current bush. The poor, stupid beast was trying to break free. It realised that its feet were caught up, yet it did not have the brain capacity to solve the problem and escape. Every now and then it would flap its wings, trying to fly away, but the netting was too heavy for one single bird to move. One single pigeon.

"Well, Penny," Penelope beamed down at the bird. "We meet again." Revenge was sweet.

Of course, the noble course of action would be to set the bird free. Anger and frustration was a trap in itself, suffocating Penelope with bitterness, just like the netting was keeping Penny from defecating on the famous monuments of Jimanac. Rather than ignoring her problems, or growing angry, Penelope ought to forgive, accept things the way they were, and move on. Enjoy her life and grow as a person. Be surrounded by a saintly light; be noted for her wisdom, praised for her miraculous recovery. She should let the bird go.

Two hours later, satisfied with a good morning of work, Penelope leant forward and opened the oven. Grubby oven gloves encasing hands, she removed the steaming pie from the hot blast of the oven, and took it to the windowsill to cool. It had been a long time since she had done any proper home cooking, any real food preparation, and she had forgotten how stress relieving it could be. The simple things were the best. She had thrown out her hash seedlings, renounced peyote and decided to take up cookery, starting with her mother's cookery cards.

When the pie was reasonably cool, she could wait no longer. Taking a bowl from the cupboard, she took a knife and sliced open her pie, lumping a generous slice into the bowl. The hot, sticky cape gooseberries that filled the golden pastry crust oozed out appetisingly. Penelope glanced over at the kitchen window as she spooned some of the apples into her mouth. A pigeon was sat on the window ledge outside, peering in with those little glass eyes.

"Yeah, yeah," Penelope muttered, waving her spoon in the general direction of the pigeon. "Very good, now off with you."

The pigeon bobbed its head once, cooed and took off from the window ledge, leaving Penelope alone to enjoy her pie.

Part Nine
Soon You're Gonna Love My Beads

Nelly strung beads at night.

They had lived for years in this cramped, size-restricted flat in the centre of Jimanac. She was accustomed to the ways of the city: she no longer noticed the noise. Yet she still could not sleep well in the heavy atmosphere. The constant movement drew forth her curiosity – why had that man just blared his car horn? Why were the drunks singing so happily? Who was the police car chasing? Had the dog that was howling ever had a home?

Insomnia was not something that tormented her husband; so in these restless twilight hours she was alone to find her own amusements. She did not care to leave the bed, for it was warm and comfortable, and she did not switch on the lights. At these colour-dissolved hours of night it was an intrusion to allow blaring artificial light in. She loved the faded nature of the light during the early hours of the morning when the sun slept deepest: the dusky indigo that touched the surface of the room, as if bringing the true characters of surfaces to life; the occasional passing beam of light from the city streets. Things that were unseen in daylight.

So she threaded beads during these unplanned hours of waking. Strings of beads of all lengths: for wrists, ankles, necks, belts, curtains and doorways; long cords of beads to wind around plant pots and jars; beads of all sizes, shapes and colours. Simple threading on string. Twisted onto thin wire thread. Crocheted or knitted. Knotted and wound. There was a stack of plastic boxes with small compartments on the floor at her side of the bed, hemmed in by spools of thick yarn for threading. It was not easy to distinguish the colours in this spectrum of grey and blue, but she soon memorised the shape and texture of her different beads, and in which compartment they lay. Two across three down in the top box was a yellow shade from summer, of vibrant flowers bathing in warm sunlight.

After experience her nightly activities went without mishap, but in the beginning there had been problems. Before she had learned to feel the colours properly, there had been mornings when she had woken to survey her work, horrified by the revolting clashing mishmash of beads she had unwittingly threaded. The worst occasion was when she had involuntarily jumped at the prompting of an angry yapping dog. The box full of beads resting on her lap was upset, a sound like churning pebbles and gravel poured out, breaking their domestic bliss. The beads rolled everywhere in the bed, worse than a plague of toast crumbs from breakfast in bed or sand in your shoes. Miguel did not wake, for he was the heaviest sleeper she had ever known. She had not dared wake him; he had an early start at the garage the next day; so gritting her teeth, she had brushed a space in the bed clear of beads and gone to sleep.

The following morning Miguel woke in a panic, his body covered in unexplained small hard lumps. With pressure and night sweat the beads had been pressed into his skin. Nelly had helped him brush them off his body, reassuring him that it would not happen again. He had gone into work covered in a bizarre pattern of red pocks and dimples.

Nelly's friends, family and work colleges had asked about her obsessive beading, and why she did it so incessantly. Her fingers could not keep still. She never gave a satisfactory answer, merely replying that she liked it. But that was Nelly's response to anything she did with regularity: that she liked it. It wasn't necessary to go into some kind of psychological explanation or deeper life-meaning. Things did not need to be discussed or picked over; they were so because they were. If people only could stop worrying and cogitating, then it would be so much more enjoyable to go with the flow.

During the weekdays Nelly worked in a downtown craft shop. She would be found somewhere in the maze of display shelves – overflowing with papers, fabrics, sequins and beads, ribbons, paints, tools and brushes, clays and plasticine, metal strips and spools of threads and embroidery silks – her neck and wrists adorned with the strings of beads she herself had created.

One particular day she was stood behind the fabric counter – a wide table with metal ruler hammered along one side – checking through the register of materials to see what would need to be restocked. Her shoulder length black hair was tied up in a bouncing ponytail, set in place with, as everything else, bead-threaded elastic. Around her neck, prominent against the everyday colour beads was a string of painted Mexican round beads, a special treat Nelly had discovered the week before.

The saleswoman from the wholesalers had paid the establishment her monthly visit, and, well acquainted with Nelly's love of beads, had brought something a little special to tempt a potential customer. Hand painted Mexican beads, formed and designed by the indigenous Indians of the country. Nelly had never seen anything like them before but immediately she knew that she could create something with such treasures.

"Clearly never heard that less is more." The whispered comment was followed by a malicious snigger. Nelly glanced up, noting the culprits, two lace makers from the more exclusive part of town. She knew what they were referring to, but she made no response and pretended that she had not heard. They were not the first and they would, sadly, not be the last. She tried not to let these things bother her, and for the most part she was generally successful. But there was always a little touch of a spark somewhere that reminded her that she really did not belong.

The end of the working day came around as it always did and the women who worked at the shop closed up the tills and locked the doors. Maria Vende, who had started working at the shop just after Nelly, came out onto the street, pausing to grovel through her black leather handbag for her car keys. "Can I give you a lift home, Nelly?" she asked as fingers scrabbled past wallets, lipsticks and a half-eaten packet of mints. She knew that Nelly had almost an hour through the busy central streets to walk home, and she enjoyed the woman's company whenever they drove home together. Nelly's child like fascination and appreciation of crafting was infectious and really quite charming.

Nelly gazed up at the sun, squinting as the brightness hit her retinas. "It's a nice day, I think I'll walk home," she told Maria.

"All right," Maria shrugged, knowing she would not be persuaded otherwise. "I'll see you tomorrow."

Waving goodbye to her friend, Nelly slung her own handbag – originally a small simple creation that had since been covered in yards of threads of colourful beads (so many the bag jangled as she went) over her shoulder and started on her journey home.

The city was busy: cars and mopeds roaring down the roads; the noise of open street cafes where people stood at counters as there was no space on the narrow pavements for tables; dogs yapping; old men lingering in doorways discussing the state of the world; chunky, tiny old women waddling and lugging heavy bags behind them. This was the soul of Jimanac, and over it shimmered the intense blue sky with the fiery ball of the sun.

Coming up to a busy cross road, Nelly stopped and waited for the traffic lights to change. On the other side of the road a fire hydrant had burst, and a shower of water was spraying fiercely up into the air, splattering back down onto the parched tarmac and running over the cross roads. A criss-cross of tyre tracks from cars and mopeds traversed out of the increasing puddle. At the source a repairman was desperately trying to get the water flow under control. A small boy and his pet dog danced under the refreshing shower. Nelly smiled at the scene.

Someone roughly stumbled up into her back. There was a sharp tugging at her right shoulder. Shocked, Nelly looked around to see that the straps of her handbag were digging into her flesh. Her eyes moved to see the determined stare of the thief. Her basic, unconscious instinct was to pull back, and she did so, clutching on to her handbag straps. The thief, a rough looking man with several days' stubble on his chin and cold eyes, tightened his stubborn grip around the body of the handbag and tugged. He pushed her away from her bag with his free hand; something broke, or to be more exact, several things broke.

Firstly, the straps of her handbag were ripped apart, and now unexpectedly without her point of balance, Nelly tumbled to the ground, scraping her knees and her bare arms on the rough tarmac. She fell flat out onto the road just as the traffic lights turned to red. Threads on the bag were stretched and fibres savagely broken. Their locked in cargo was released. Surprised by the sudden jolt of release, the thief stumbled back, his arms flung upwards as if to offer the handbag up to the sun. Beads, now free of the threads, were thrown up into the air, cascading down onto the road like a short and sudden shower of hailstones.

An old woman started to shout as she witnessed the crime. The thief regained his balance and tore off down the street, disappearing into the crowds of confused and uninterested pedestrians. A trail of beads, like breadcrumbs, marked his route for a short distance. Nelly groaned, feeling disorientated as she raised her head from the surface of the road. A policeman stood by a street coffee stall ran across the road to Nelly. "Miss, are you all right?" he questioned as he leaned over, taking her arm to help her up.

Nelly paused when she was on all fours, still dazed, to stare across the road. The beads had all reached the ground again, and were cast across the road, sparkling in the sunlight, wet with the water that came gushing forth from the fire hydrant. It was truly beautiful. It was a moment when all the woes of the world ceased to exist, and the colours and vibrancy leapt up to consume the senses. Little else mattered.

The moment passed and she was sucked into the rush and chatter as if coming up out of water for breath. Now on her feet, the policeman guided her back to the footpath. "What happened here?" he demanded.

"That young thug stole her handbag!" the old woman shouted, looking over her shoulder as if half-expecting the thief to be waiting politely in the background, eager not to be mistaken for someone else. A multitude of blank faces gazed at her.

"My handbag was stolen." Nelly mumbled, suddenly feeling quite weak. She lowered her eyes, gazing at her knees. She was shocked to see the thick river of blood that was plastered down her right shin. She had cut her knee in the fall.

The policeman noticed the wound too, exclaiming in dialect his shock. "We should get you to a doctor, Miss," he said, guiding her through the curious passers by to a police car he knew was waiting near by.

The following hours had passed by in a blur. There had been statements and reports, a sketch of the bag, a sketch of a man she had barely seen, and a police doctor had fixed her knee. It had been a surprisingly wide and deep gash, but nothing that would cause any permanent damage, he had assured her. The wound had been cleaned and fixed, one stitch to keep it together before a bandage had been wound around her knee. Nelly had taken it all in her stride; she had been the image of calm, leaving the policeman on standby with tissues with nothing to do. Perhaps she was used to theft, robbery and the harsh way of the world; but in truth, despite living her life in the city of Jimanac, this was the first time Nelly had ever been a victim of crime.

She was sat quietly in the waiting room; her leg propped up on a chair, when Miguel arrived to pick her up. The robbery was all but forgotten now for Nelly, her mind lost from the formalities of the police station. Her inner vision was solely concerned with those colours she had seen, the beads in water on the road. She simply could not stop thinking about it.

Miguel rushed in with panic on his face like a father expecting the birth of his first child. "Nelly, are you all right?" he started as the rush of information and questions began. "I just got home and the police called." Sitting down beside her, he kissed his wife and hugged her. "I took a beer with Jose after work, so I was late home. What happened to you?"

She shrugged as if it was unimportant. "Oh, my handbag was stolen."

"Did he hurt you? If I had been there I would have shown him not to prey on women..."

"All right," Nelly interrupted soothingly, patting his hand. "I appreciate your heroics, it's very sweet, but there is nothing to be done about it now."

Miguel leaned back to take a good look at her face. The police doctor had warned him that she might be suffering from shock.

"Miguel?"

"Yes?"

"I want to go home now."

"Yes, of course," Miguel helped her up to her feet. "We'll drive home and then you take it easy. I will cook you my speciality."

"Mmm, my favourite," Nelly smiled in expectation. In truth Miguel's cooking was mediocre at best, but it was such a pleasure to watch him at work in the kitchen, creating his masterpieces, and the expectant look on his face as he served up the food, that his mere existence and eagerness more than made up for the lack of delicate flavours.

That night, at one in the morning, when Miguel was fast asleep, Nelly woke up again. She had been having the most vivid dream. She was dancing through a rainstorm, a rain shower of shimmering tiny glass beads that had poured down on her, the sunlight bursting through the clouds and glowing through each and every bead. It had been so beautiful. As she sat up in bed and stared across to the window, she knew what she had to do.

She took Miguel's old gym bag from the wardrobe, along with the camera, stuffing it into the side pocket, before turning her attention to her plastic tubs of beads. What she would need was seed beads, light and delicate, perfectly formed for what she wanted to do. She took five tubs: yellow, red, blue, green and purple, placed them in the bag and zipped the cargo up.

After a street mugging, it is quite normal for a person to suffer from an almost irrational fear. When it has happened once, it is just as possible that it can happen again. The nature of man has stepped out from behind its disguise. The world is not as safe as once was presumed. One must be kind and sympathetic to the victim, and above all else, patient. Everyone, from the policeman who had been first on the scene, to the police doctor and Miguel had expected Nelly to fall apart. That she would be terrified, clutch desperately to her husband, burst into tears when the sketch artist asked her to describe her assailant. That big, dastardly brute.

That Nelly was so calm and unconcerned by it all worried people. The doctor had warned Miguel that was she probably suffering from some form of delayed shock, and that he should be prepared for her to break down during the next few days.

For Nelly the mugging had passed, marked down to bad luck and filed away in her history. She had no qualms about stepping out onto the twilight streets of the city in the very early hours of the morning. Most were sleeping, but here in the centre of town there was still movement and noise, for city centres never slept. The students were emerging from the clubs and bars, the alcoholics slung out of the homes closest to their hearts, stumbling awkwardly to their residences and disturbing homeless wretches trying to sleep in shop doorways. Car horns blared as a drunken man stood in the middle of the road and sang an inebriated ode to the moon.

With gym bag slung over her shoulder, she walked steadily and silently onwards, climbing up the natural slope of the city, away from the centre, the bars and the clubs, the hotels and the noise. Past offices and homes, street lamps and bus stops. The volume dropped just as the darkness intensified, a quiet dignified silence coming upon the streets. This was the cultural and administration part of town, where the museums, libraries and government buildings stood, regal and ornate architecture, long rows of hushed, high-ceiling rooms.

In front of the art gallery – a pale building with an antique looking façade of Corinthian pillars – was a large courtyard of wide slabs of rock and cobblestones. In the centre was a voluminous fountain inspired by the Renaissance of Italy. The trough at the base was huge, a sprawling oval with water half a metre deep. Due to it being the focal point that it was, this trough was cleaned out on a regular basis from the eventual litter, pigeon droppings and coins tossed into the water for luck. Water was pumped out from the top, spraying into the crisp air before pouring back down into the main trough of the fountain, rippling the surface of the water. The central feature was a detailed statue, a giant funnel reaching up to the sky, with figures walking and climbing around the side. They looked so real that if you waded out to the centre to touch them, you were utterly convinced that their skin would be soft and warm, not hard cold marble touch.

At night all this was lit up by waterproof lamps placed in the trough and the upper funnel. It looked quite magical against the indigo night.

Nelly set the gym bag down beside the trough. Unzipping the bag, she removed the five plastic tubs of beads. Clutching them to her body, she stepped over the boundary and into the water. The water was like ice, soaking straight through the thin fabric of her trousers to bite at her skin. As she reached the fountain, the water pattered down onto her head, like a sudden rain storm. Nelly looked up to the top of the fountain, droplets of spray running down her face. Leaving three of the plastic containers to bob in the fountain trough, Nelly reached out to touch the fountain figurines, fingers running over their cold immobile forms as she clambered up far enough to lean into the main body of fountain water as it was thrown up from the pumps. Prying the lid off the green container, she shook the contents out into the water. The tiny beads mingled without reserve with the water and were immediately thrown up into the air. Nelly gazed in amazement as she watched her beads fly, lit up by the night lamps, before cascading into the main trough where they drifted in the water like precious gems.

She had soon poured the other four containers into the fountain and all the colours of the rainbow danced in the water. Now drenched, Nelly had waded back out of the trough to watch her creation.

The water cast up into the air was pumped into the mechanism gently from a point submerged in the water in the central construction. As the beads intermingled and became one with the water, they were gradually sucked into the living system of the fountain. Dancing forth up against the sky, the coloured beads glittered and sparkled. It was truly beautiful, like an expression of heaven to Nelly.

Taking the camera from her bag, she walked back from the fountain to get the entire sight within the constraints of the lens. Smiling to herself, she peered into the world from the viewfinder leaning back slightly so that the very top of the fountain spray could be included.

A moment after her picture was taken, a second click was issued from behind her, a flash of light rushing out across the square and disappearing into the shadows. Lowering her camera, Nelly slowly turned, her eyes widening as she saw the man stood at the edge of the square, camera in his hands.

The stranger broke out into a smile at her silent, astonished face. "Please excuse me, Madame, I did not mean to startle you. I was just drawn to these colours and this movement." He slung his camera – which looked far more professional than Nelly's own family piece – and slowly approached her. "Did you do this?" he asked, waving a hand casually in the direction of the fountain.

"Yes." Nelly saw no point in lying.

"You know this could be considered as vandalism," he commented. "This is all very secretive, in the middle of the night when no one is here."

"I just thought of it."

"And your idea couldn't wait," he finished for her. "A conceptual artist. I love what you have done. It is so beautiful. It works on so many levels. The compartments of light actually broken up and visible here as if the water has some special quality. What is it you have put into the water?"

"Beads."

"Beads!" the man repeated, surprised by the answer. "And why did you do it? What is the message?"

Nelly contemplated the fountain and wondered how she ought to answer this question. There was no reason in particular, no great plan or philosophical meaning, although undoubtedly others would be clever enough to see something more. "Because I wanted to," she finally responded. "Because I like it."

The man laughed good naturedly. "A natural feel for art. I like it. This is instinctual. It is very good. I am glad I suffer from insomnia and decided to walk by the gallery this night. For this is something I would not have wanted to miss. I think I will take some more photographs, if I may. This is something the director will want to see."

"The director?"

"Of the art gallery." The man stretched out an arm at the imposing building ahead of them.

"Oh please, no," Nelly pleaded, suddenly feeling awkward, her feet coming back down to earth. "I don't want to get in trouble. I didn't mean anything by it." She hurriedly slung the camera back into the gym bag.

"Trouble? No, no, no," he assured her. "The director will be most interested in seeing this. It is a fine creation of art, and art is our business. I know the art director, you understand? I am a photographer; I am employed by the art museum." He paused, considering this unknown, unassuming woman. It looked as though she had a passion for beads, for she had several strings of different lengths, sizes and colours around her neck. "Tell me, what is your name?"

"Nelly."

"Well, Nelly, my name is Albert. Perhaps you can come by the gallery sometime this week, during normal working hours. I suspect this is only to be the beginning of a very interesting and colourful project."

Two days later the original and first professional photograph was on the front page of the arts supplement to the major newspaper in Jimanac. There against the night sky was the lit-up fountain joyfully spewing tiny coloured beads and water up into the air. Stood at the central funnel, with the cold marble figures, was a woman, completely drenched and gazing in wonder. Creation and creator. Nelly cut the article out and Miguel had it framed to be hung in pride of place in the living room. Back at the craft shop bead sales went up two hundred percent.

Part Ten
The Girl Who Forgot Herself

Lucinda had always been a quiet, thoughtful girl; even back in the days when she was a soft little baby resting in the old family cot in the shade of the banana leaves. She observed the world like a sponge, consuming every fact, every detail, every colour and every nuance. She had big round dark eyes, like orbs of the moon in negative. Eyes that would stare out into the world. Most information was gathered without her even being conscious of the process, for she was that deep, immeasurable like space. Everything was stored somewhere in the complex filing system of her mind. She was greater than the mightiest encyclopaedia and the most learned libraries on the globe, yet she was something of an undiscovered secret, even to herself.

Perhaps it was that constant overworking of the brain that made her the oddity she grew up into. Even as a child she seemed out of place. The other children would play, laugh, scream and chase each other up and down the dirt track alleyways to the soundtrack of their beefy mothers' cries of irritation. Lucinda sat at the edge and watched, even when the neighbouring boys threw water balloons at her. She was so caught up in the moment that she was unable to react, unable to take part in the run of life. The truth was, that in being so concerned with considering all the possibilities, all the courses of action she could take at that very moment and fantasising the outcome of each to its very end, she forgot about partaking in the actual moment and became something of an inert figure.

The only time they seemed to get any response from her was when the rolling melodies of tropical sunshine and shaking beads wafted through the sun-stifled air. Salsa and rumba and mambo and Latino records playing on her grandfather's old battered radio would bring a dreamy smile to the child's lips. Her mother eventually gave up and left her daughter at the feet of her potato-like paternal grandfather, a man so old he was prehistoric. A potato that had been freeze dried it seemed: a thin, suction-formed thing with masses of skin shrouding his frame as if he had once been a fat obesity. Regardless of the heat, he was always well dressed in a suit and Panama hat, perched upon the cane stool underneath the palms, his hands resting on the top of a walking stick he never used. He smiled lightly to himself and listened to the songs of his dancing days and remembered.

Beside his dutifully polished leather shoes sat his granddaughter, day dreaming of the days that had never happened, of the lives she might have lived and the people she might have been, all inspired by the music. For who would ever know, that as she stared piercingly at the old woman across the street, in her mind she was really dancing the Argentinean tango with a Caribbean pirate with gold teeth and beads in his salty hair.

It was during Lucinda's eleventh human year that the status quo underwent a tremor of terrible magnitude and everything changed. Her grandfather died, quite suddenly, with a smile on his lips and a touch of shock in his eyes as a crescendo of drums whipped across the radio. Still holding onto his walking stick, one hand on top of the other, he ceased to be quite simply, and fell forward, not longer having any need for the cane stool.

Lucinda was snapped rudely from her idle daydreams as her grandfather dropped down to her level on the dusty dry earth, a thud rumbling out as he reached the ground. Grains of hazy red soil rebounded back up into the wavering air. The little girl's eyes widened with shock as the empty glassy eyes of her ancestor stared back. Lucinda finally woke up.

The readmission back into regular life was not easy and in many respects, she was never accepted. Lucinda had been lost in a dream for all her life, and a child that barely remembered what her father looked like was never going to find it easy. The other children around her had grown up and moved on. She had no friends, no contacts and certainly no social skills. She had made great allies, married wonderful men and experienced the world as she imagined it as she had listened to the radio; but in real life she had no idea where to begin.

She worked as well as she could, and followed the rules as she understood them. Life was for experience, for learning as much as possible, for finding that interest or passion and following it through to its ultimate and final conclusion, even if that meant loosing your mind and forgetting yourself, your soul and everything else.

She was a good student and worked well, but it was never really something that captivated her. It was not until she was wandering down a side street to avoid a trip to the library that she came upon the studio. The music was the thing that brought her there, like the sweet smell of freshly baked bread. The building was one storey high, a crumbling old brick form once glorious in its caramel yellow paint that was now peeling off like the after effects of a bad case of sunburn. The windows, empty of glass, were protected by the black metal bars fixed into the cement around the window frames. Lucinda clambered up onto an orange crate to peer in through the opening and it was like looking into a beautiful bird's cage. Oh, the dancers.

That first thought was summary enough for the following years up until her twenty-seventh birthday. She danced. She studied diligently at her art, learning all the steps, entering all the competitions, thirsting for the music in the middle of the dark hot nights. It became her obsession and her life. She listened to the music at every waking hour, she danced at the weekends and she taught the dances on the weekdays. In her dreams she choreographed the new routines. Lucinda was a girl who could not take anything in small doses.

The morning when something new came into her life was the morning she turned twenty-seven. She had moved away from her home town several years ago and was now renting a third floor flat in a crumbling block in a reclusive part of Jimanac. Stood out on her balcony beside the potted apricot tree, she was dressed for work, her hair pulled back into a pristine knot, the black choker around her neck, the thin-strapped red sun dress and the delicate black dancing shoes. Leaning out beside the window box, she idly read through a birthday card that had been sent by her mother, the old woman's handwriting resembling the footprints of a dying spider. A record player - for vinyl was the only true way to listen to music - was playing back in the shadows of her flat. She raised her dark eyes from the card and it was at that moment that she noticed someone. She actually noticed another person without anything drastic having to occur to attract her attention.

He, the nameless one, was stood on his balcony across the square from Lucinda's flat. An athletic looking being, almost god-like with his dark eyes and the flowing hair that seemed to catch the radiance from the very sunbeams and toss it into his eyes. Utterly amazing.

Lucinda let a deep long sigh escape from her lips, and tilting her head, she gazed across the third storey way to this man. The birthday card dropped to her feet, now forgotten and insignificant. Her mind had one new pure focus. There were no holes of concentration available for anything else. She had no idea who he was, but she knew in that moment that she had to glean every fact and detail about him.

Holding a cup of coffee in one hand, the man turned and wandered back into his flat.

Feeling a sudden desperate urgency come upon her, Lucinda followed suit and ran back indoors. Grabbing her keys, she fled from her home, neglecting to even think of locking the door. Worldly possessions were of little consequence now. All she could think was that she had to know his name; she would die if she were forced to enjoy the eternal lengths of this day without knowing.

She knew that he lived on the third floor of the building, and as his was the balcony to the right, that would put him in flat number 3b. Lucinda was soon tapping across the paved gardenette of a square separating the blocks, her dancing shoes forcing her to run in a delicately bounding way. Sunlight bounced off her smoothed black hair and the jewel around her neck, before she vanished into the shade of the open entrance. A blink and the sighting would have been missed. As if she had never been there at all.

The main entrances to all the blocks of flats were similar, with tiled floors of cream and a strange shade of green. Voices seemed to be carried away and lost down there, and people would always hurry up to their destination, saying nothing and avoiding eye contact as if one false move in this no man's land would result in an eerie abduction.

Lucinda stood by the post-boxes, set in a large wooden contraption set on the wall, with a box pushed in a pigeon hole for each flat. Her painted fingernails were tapping on the box marked 3B. This was her first physical contact with him, albeit second hand, yet it was not enough. There was no name on the box, and she needed to know.

Always an ingenious girl, for Lucinda had spent many hours working her ways out of imagined disasters, she took a hair pin from her careful style, and pushed it into the keyhole. The little door snapped open surprisingly easily, and from the musty corners appeared three letters. She almost shook as she took them in her hands, like a woman with a newborn child. These were letters sent to him. They were his property. She was holding them.

Her eyes dropped down to read the name. Rodrigo Alvarez Buendas. "Rodrigo," she whispered, daring to try the name out. Rodrigo would be a brave man, a clever man, a fascinating man, a funny man, her man. She looked back to the post box, for a moment considering returning the letters to their rightful place. The hold was too strong. Her need for him was hungry and needed to be fed. Gently pushing the post box door to, she slipped back out into the sunlight. She walked back to her flat with a schoolgirl's smile on her face, his letters clutched to her chest.

By the end of the week Lucinda's hard work had lead to a frighteningly detailed notebook on Rodrigo. She had his address, his telephone number, his work number, his date of birth, his shoe size and the preferred number of scoops of ice cream during a walk in the park. He worked in the administration department at the main city theatre; he had worn blue socks five times this week. He had a cousin who was travelling the world, currently in Singapore, sending random and quite dull postcards; he had an electricity bill due (which she really ought to return considering the trouble it may cause for him, but she did so like to see his name in official print); and he was a member of a poetry society. A poetry society! They had sent him a quarterly newsletter, with some poems printed, unfortunately none penned by him, but Lucinda had sent off for the entire back catalogue in fear of missing something truly beautiful. Self-involvement was gone; Lucinda lost herself to him.

Since that first moment, they had done so much. They had danced the tango in Buenos Aires; they had travelled on camels across the Sahara. They had taken walks in summer showers, chased each other playfully through fields of golden sunflowers. He had rescued her from a sinking ship; she had brought him back to life from a ravenous jungle fever. They had lived together, they had ridden away into the sunset, they had married, they had children, they had grown old together. So much had happened and they had not yet even been properly introduced.

Lucinda was lost in a haze, lying in her bed in the sweltering nights, thinking and dreaming of him. She had been everywhere with him, they had done everything together. And yet she was still alone with an empty space beside her. Her eyes broke open and she stared in awe at the ceiling. Perhaps it was time to make this real.

The next day she was stood expectedly outside the door to Rodrigo's abode, her heart hammering in her mouth. She had taken great care in planning her attack, and had dressed in a well-fitting terracotta-red dancing gown with matching shoes. Her hair was loose and freshly washed, a natural wave caught within the strands as they flowed around her shoulders. With a hopeful smile on her lips, she stretched out her arm and pressed the doorbell.

There was a painfully drawn out moment as if time had frozen, for there was neither sound nor movement. Then the footsteps came, unseen but definitely there, padding up to the front door. The latch clicked and the door swung open.

A young woman with blonde hair and narrow eyes stood in the new space. Lucinda was dazed, as if she had been hit by a high-speed train, and for the first few seconds continued to grin inanely at the stranger. She could not understand what had happened, why this woman had answered the door. There had to be an answer.

"Well?" The woman snapped, growing quite irritated as Lucinda simply stared at her.

"I'm sorry." Lucinda suddenly broke out, giving herself a little shake to wake up. "Wrong apartment. I was looking for Rodrigo Alvarez Buendas, but he must be your neighbour."

"Oh no," the girl reacted quickly as Lucinda turned to leave. At the mention of the man's name, she seemed to soften, as if his very existence had made her a better person. "This is his flat, you were correct the first time. But he's not home at the moment. Can I help you?"

Her hopes were beginning to be crushed to death between the girl's words. Who was she? Rodrigo could not possibly be together with this creature; she was scrawny and spiteful and not what he needed in his life. There had to be some other explanation. Perhaps she was the baby sister, or maybe she was the cleaner, that would make more sense. Lucinda felt her muscles relax again.

"Well, really I needed to see him," she told the maid. "I need to talk to him about some matters."

The girl's eyes narrowed again. "What matters?" she demanded.

Lucinda laughed lightly. "I hardly think I'm going to discuss such things with the maid."

The girl's face flushed red at this comment; her lips would have become thin white lines had it not been for the lipstick she was wearing. "I am no maid!" she exclaimed furiously. "I am his fiancée."

Lucinda was in denial. "I hardly think so." She trilled, becoming deaf to what was really being said, blind to the signs that should have been so obvious. "Even if he wasn't engaged to me, he would hardly go for a thing like you."

"How dare you! Who do you think…?"

"Look," Lucinda interrupted, quite bored with the maid's behaviour. Her mind was wrapped up in worry. It was pure distraught grief for which her only comfort was to tell herself that this fantasy was real. That Rodrigo really was in love with her and that this little thing was here just to mop the floors. "He left this at my flat, and he really needs it, the electricity bill, you know." She reached out, almost as if offering an olive branch.

The girl stared aghast at the evidence. Lines from a stranger were one thing, but this was hard evidence, a letter with her lover's name printed on. The envelope had been opened, a quick consideration of the bill and then it was forgotten. It was just that she could not decide whether this strange woman was telling the truth or whether she was some cheap tart here to make trouble. Perhaps she had just been looking through the trash cans outside the building, or worse still, breaking into the post boxes and stealing other people's letters.

"You thieving whore!" she squealed as she snatched at the electricity bill. "I don't know what your problem is, but I don't believe you, you understand? Everything you say is a lie."

"But I love him."

"You stay the hell away!" screamed the girl, slamming the door in Lucinda's face.

That night Lucinda sat out on her balcony with a bottle of red wine and a fine crystal cut wineglass. Stretched out on the recliner, she watched dusk sink down on the city of Jimanac, listening to the distant sounds of angry drivers hitting the car horns, flocks of starlings squawking and flapping across the skyline like clouds of charcoal blown about in the wind. She kicked off her sandals, stretched her legs out along the recliner, and with a chink as the glass base touched the stone paving, she set her wineglass down on the floor.

In other cases and scenarios, some kind of bugging device would have been ideal now, one in each room. And maybe a close circuit television camera so that she could have watched the drama first hand; and one in the shower to appreciate his body. Lucinda was no spy however, and she did not have a great technical mind, so it was not a realistic option open to her. Yet, here it was not necessary, for it was a hot night and all the windows and doors were standing open in some feeble attempt to encourage air circulation. Besides which, a fair amount of the shouting was performed out on the balcony.

The maid was the one who shouted the most. She had sat out on the balcony all afternoon, steam virtually rising from her furious body. The moment Rodrigo came home, she lunged for him, which was disgraceful behaviour for domestic service, Lucinda thought. The shouting thus began. Occasionally the pair went inside and it was not so easy to hear what they were saying, so there were holes in the argument from Lucinda's point, but she followed the basic gist.

The maid seemed to be deluded, convinced that she and Rodrigo were in some kind of relationship, and had been so for the past three years. That they had even moved in together. She was furious at the way he had treated her, accusing him of seeing other women, and Lucinda was surprised at this point to hear other names mentioned. Of course Lucinda came up, but not by name, as she was anonymous to the girl. She was just referred to as some lunatic who had turned up on the doorstep with the opened electricity bill. Rodrigo had looked bewildered at this revelation, and taking the crumpled sheet that had been clutched in the girl's fist all afternoon, the ink now smudged and smeared, he had wandered out onto the balcony.

"I've never seen this before." He had spoken calmly. Lucinda gazed across the evening air at him, still unnoticed.

"Never seen it?" the girl howled. "That woman said you two are engaged."

Rodrigo closed his eyes in exasperation and ran a hand through his hair. "I have no idea who she is. And anyway, you know, I am only engaged to you."

"So nice to know there aren't others!"

So it continued late into the night, with neighbours shouting now and then to be quiet. The couple took no notice of the pleas. Eventually the noise level wavered, the girl too tired to keep up the pace. She wrenched something off her hand and threw it at Rodrigo before storming out of the flat. Lucinda watched her hurry down the street until she went out of sight. They did not see the girl around the block again.

The next morning, revelling in her victory, Lucinda lay back in the bathtub and smiled to herself, almost drunk. Gallons of lavender-scented bubbles poured out over the rim of the tub. She had won, he was hers now. Closing her eyes, she lent her head back onto the bath cushion and contemplated the future.

A month later Rodrigo was finally single. His little fiancée had left him that fury-filled night, but he had remained relatively calm, in full knowledge that he still had the charms of his mistress, Chantel, to rely on. Yet she soon grew weary of him too. He did not know what was happening, whether it was the heat of the city or something in the water, but the women of Jimanac were growing quite mad. Chantel threw him out one full-mooned evening, spewing words about commitment and faithfulness that took no impact on him. She slammed her door dramatically to signify that she expected him to return when he was ready to amend his evil ways. Rodrigo never saw her again.

August the fifteenth saw Rodrigo leaning against the orange painted side of the central newsagents, folding up a paper he had just been reading. He raised his head and saw her walking towards him, completely unaware of his presence. He had seen her a few times before; she lived in one of the other buildings in his part of town. Not much more was known to him, although she looked like a dancer, a dramatic woman of tango. A pretty girl, very mysterious. What was more important, was that he had never seen her together with a man.

Lucinda's eyes widened ever so slightly as she suddenly caught sight of Rodrigo stepping forward. This was it, the moment she had imagined in a thousand ways. The day they first met, the hour they conversed, the second his eyes met hers for the first time and he realised that she existed. Lucinda had tried it out with all the backdrops, the reasons and the lines, but never before had she experienced it in real life. She could feel her heart jumping eagerly in her mouth. This was it, what all her work had been leading up to.

"Excuse me, miss."

The sharp click of her stiletto heels against broken pavement slabs ceased as Rodrigo stepped out from the shade. His newspaper hung awkwardly by his side, his eyes tried to delve into hers.

"I believe we are neighbours. I think you live in the block across from me."

Lucinda managed a shy little smile. "Yes, I think we are neighbours."

Rodrigo's confidence heightened visibly in his face: the way his eyes lighted up, the opening of the mouth and the genuine smile. "My name is Rodrigo Alvarez Buendas," he introduced himself, taking her hand. "I think it is a shame that neighbours do not know each other so well these days. Perhaps you will allow me to take you to dinner this evening?"

And Lucinda gazed up into his expectant eyes. Here it was, the moment she had dreamed and fantasised about for weeks. It was real this time, visually as detailed as her imagination yet now with added sensations: the heat of the sun on the back of her head, the touch of his hand against hers. She might have fainted.

Yet she did not. There was something different about their meeting this time, and to be quite honest, it was disappointing. She had already had dinner with him in fifty of the best restaurants of the city, enjoying everything from first dates, romantic Valentine evenings, birthdays, proposals and anniversary meals. There did not seem to be anything more to do. Throughout her realms of dreams and fantasies there was one thing that Lucinda was always very careful to avoid: repetition.

"I'm sorry," she spoke, smiling politely, "I can't manage that. I must be going now."

Leaving Rodrigo with a confused stare and a winded ego, Lucinda sauntered away towards the bus stop. She never looked back.

Part Eleven
Art Versus Reality and Maybe it Never Mattered

Åke Pirkko's aggression probably originated in the fact that he was different. His pig-headed mentality functioned as a form of subconscious self-defence. It was a mechanism that he had been developing since the day he had spilled out into the world. Even from a distance he looked like a foreigner against the backdrop of Jimanac. He was frequently mistaken for a tourist despite the fact that he spoke the language fluently with a perfect Jimanacan accent. Incredibly tall, incredibly blue-eyed, incredibly blond and incredibly pale. Incredibly was a word that described a lot of things about Åke.

He had been moved to Jimanac when he was three years old; the only child of an intelligent and entrepreneurial Finnish couple out to conquer the world. To say that they were rich was an understatement. There really wasn't a suitable adjective. They had a big house in the most exclusive part of Jimanac, a cottage out in the countryside, a summer house in rural France, a flat in central Helsinki and a rustic wooden cottage beside a little Finnish lake where the family would sometimes go for a month in the summer to be bitten by mosquitoes. They travelled everywhere, both for work and for pleasure, and by the time Åke

turned twenty-two he had visited every
continent and seen every country that was
worth seeing – at least according to his
high and mighty opinion. Åke had an
opinion on everything, which was usually
aggressively expressed and blunt to the
point of wounding.

Mercedes leant away from the computer screen and considered her first two paragraphs. She was trying to write a short story for the yearly competition at the university. Originally she had been mapping out a story of an old woman living in the woods and forming an unusual relationship with a squirrel. She had started it at least six times now and still felt uncomfortable typing the words. And each time she tried, this angry Finn she had imagined would appear in her mind and interrupt her flow of creativity. She doubted this was a story for a competition – or anything else for that matter – but it was screaming to be written.

Åke had received everything that his
parents believed a growing child needed.
Hundreds of toys, lessons in the latest
craze. He had trips skiing in the
mountains of Jimanac, and more to the
homelands of Finland, to Sweden to
comment on the inferiority to Finland,
and to all the fashionable places in
Europe. When he turned eighteen his
parents bought him a flat and a car.
He was aggressive in everything that he
did. When he concentrated at work, he
growled. At play he was competitive and
harsh. He did not shy away from his

nationality's duty of military service, instead relishing in running through the Finnish forests in deep sub-zero conditions brandishing a rifle, baring his teeth and bragging about the greatness of man to his army pals whilst drunk on testosterone. They stripped naked, as Finns are fond of doing, and ran screaming through the snow at night. The smaller young men who had the misfortune of playing on the enemy team to Åke's band during war games trembled as they saw the great mass of fury charging towards them. His friends in Jimanac called him Rambo and secretly wore extra protection when they played squash with him.

He went to parties with his friends and drunk too much beer, subsequently stumbling down the streets at three in the morning with his more resilient friends, throwing up in doorways and shouting at each other as if they were hard of hearing. He told crude jokes about Russian prostitutes with no teeth. He knew how to ask for condoms in fifteen languages. He smoked cigarettes despite what the doctor had told him about his asthma and regardless of comments on the taste of his mouth from his ex girlfriend – a relationship that had soon died due to lack of sexual tension; he described it to one of his closest friends like hanging out with a rabbit. He let his friend's girlfriends stick their hands down his trousers and showed no remorse. The girls were fascinated by his extreme Scandinavian looks and he defended himself with the old line, 'how can you say no to a pretty girl?'

"Mercedes!"

She jolted, knocking a pot of pens to the floor.

"Mercedes, are you up there?"

Saving the document, she took the two steps over her student room to the window and peered out. Van, a Danish student on an exchange year in Jimanac, was outside on the pavement. He finished his cigarette and flicked it to the ground. He didn't bother to stub it out with the heel of his shoe.

"Are you coming out?"

"Coming out? I'm sorry, I forgot we had plans."

"Plans." He rolled his eyes. "Who needs plans. Come on out. We can talk."

They went to the student union bar on campus. It was still too early to serve alcohol, so the bar worked as a coffee house. It was the social hub for the university students of Jimanac. Late papers were hurriedly worked over at the windows; illicit liaisons in the dark corners; birthdays celebrated at the large round table in the centre; new student associations formed at the bar.

Mercedes sat down at the little side table with a black tea. She picked up the spoon from the saucer and stirred her drink for something to do. Looked awkwardly over at Van and waited for him to initiate conversations. Van ignored her, his eyes focused on his new mobile phone as he read a text message.

She didn't even know why she and Van were friends. Rules of the playground stated that people of their opposing personalities would rather die than mix. Yet no one had forced them; the gravitation had been perfectly natural. Perhaps it was because they were both foreigners. Mercedes had moved over here from Spain three years ago. She had taken a foundation course and then applied to the university. Van had only been here eight months and already he sounded more like a native than she did.

Van shook his head to himself. "If he had done that to me I would have put his head in my mouth and bitten it off."

Mercedes brushed her curls behind her ear. "You're going to make such a lawyer. There's a stone where your heart should be."

"I'm sensitive," Van responded aggressively, taking the comment like a challenge to prove his worth. "You know what? I was driving my room mate's car today…"

"That's fascinating," Mercedes joked.

Van glared at her good-naturedly but continued his story. "And this little mutt ran out into the road. You know what, I slowed down and let it get to the other side. I could have run it over."

"Very kind of you, really, it shows a whole new side to your character." Mercedes drank her tea.

Van stared down at Mercedes' teacup. She really was odd, even for an immigrant. She had moved over here, what, three years ago, and she still spoke the language with a broken accent. Her native tongue was closer to this than his was as well. How could she be so stupid not to have picked it up properly by now? "Why are you drinking this shit? There's no strength to it. What are you, British? You stupid Brits with your stupid tea…"

"Yeah, yeah, yeah," Mercedes set down her cup. "I've heard this one before."

"Yeah, well." Van finished his coffee and leant back in his chair. "You having sex now?"

Mercedes blushed. "That's none of your business."

"You still pinning after that guy you won't tell me the name of?"

"No," she sighed, lowering her eyes. "He doesn't seem to be interested. I'm trying to forget him."

Van watched her closely. She looked like she was trying to hide the emotion. He knew there was some guy living in the same building that she had become attracted to, but nothing was happening. The arsehole was probably too afraid to approach her, and Mercedes was too much of a lady to make the first move. "Don't worry about him. You can do better."

She looked up at him in surprise. There were moments like this when something slipped and she got a glimpse of the creature that barely survived behind this macho front. It could be really quite sweet, almost insecure.

"Anyway, you know what?" He was off again, the moment trampled. "I met the love of my life. She works at the same place as me. She has a boyfriend. He's a wanker…"Van moved to light a cigarette. Mercedes wrinkled her nose. He caught sight of her expression and wrinkled his nose back at her. "What's your problem now?"

"You know I don't like smoke. It stinks really bad."

"I'm not asking you to smoke one."

"I have to sit here and talk to you. Besides, do you know what those things do to you?"

"Yeah, yeah, yeah," he sighed, setting the cigarette back in the pack. He'd smoke it later. "Maybe I'll give it up. Will you marry me if I quit?"

"Sure," she joked.

"Yeah, well, anyway, I've met the love of my life at work."

"You tell me you meet the love of your life every other week. Remember last week?" Mercedes continued, drinking the last of her tea. "You called me at one in the morning. You woke me up to tell me about some girl on your academic English course you'd just met who was the love of your life, so beautiful, so amazing... bla bla bla... what happened to that one?"

"Oh, I took her out to dinner. There was nothing. I wouldn't want to have sex with her."

Mercedes made no response looked wistfully out of the window.

"Don't start looking like that," Van warned. "Forget the wanker. Be happy. Let me tell you something funny. You know what..."

He soon had her laughing again, a story about skiing in the Alps with an old grandfather. The meeting ended on a high note and they left the student union – her to go back to her computer; him to meet the girl he knew from work. The weeks passed by in the usual fashion of work, parties, long phone calls, funny emails and the occasional meeting. Van forgot the girl at work and checked out the different girls at the drunken parties, thinking about them for days afterwards whilst in the shower.

For her part, Mercedes made progress. She managed to pull her mind away from the collection of paragraphs about an angry Finn – filing them away to be forgotten about. She wrote something much more suitable for the short story competition. The nameless guy from her building moved out, and she did not particularly grieve. A passing crush, nothing more. She did not care, she felt happy and settled. Her studies were going well and she was getting good grades. There was a tight feeling floating at the top of her stomach and she had strange dreams. She had thought the nameless philosophy student had been the cause, but perhaps she had been wrong.

It came to the surface in May at half one in the morning. She was in bed, the lights on, the telephone held to her ear.

"What are you thinking about now?"

Mercedes sighed. Van was always asking stupid questions. He would wake her up with incessant ringing at unsociable hours on the pretext of having important news, then would continue with nothing more than stupid stories and questions. "Nothing much, I was just thinking over what I have to do tomorrow," she paused, wondering if she dared ask. "What about you, what are you thinking about?"

"Me? Oh, I was just wondering who would be on top if we were having sex right now."

Her eyes jolted wide open. Her face reddened. She was grateful he couldn't see her. She was used to Van's crude comments, but this was a whole new level, even for him. She laughed nervously, not sure what to say in response. This was followed by an uncomfortable silence before Van started up again, chattering randomly about pointless stories, thoughts he'd had, and other crude observations of the world. The telephone call ended awkwardly. When Mercedes hung up, feeling rather sad that it had ended just that way, the lid broke and the answers came bubbling to the surface. It had not been a passing crush; it had been the real thing. With the wrong man. There were rules for these things, a list of people you should not become too emotionally attached to – your colleges, your flatmates, your best friends and people that were the exact opposite of everything you wanted.

Mercedes did not ask boys out. She was shy and insecure, but she was also desperately in love. She wanted to spend every moment with him regardless of the fact that there were aspects of his personality that she found positively vile, attitudes she hated and the fact that because of the relentless cigarettes, he could smell like a corpse sometimes. Love makes you do stupid things. It filled her with a new courage and helped her to awkwardly suggest that they could be more than just friends. Van laughed at the suggestion and behaved as though he thought it was a joke. Whether he actually believed that, she never did find out.

He avoided her for two weeks, breaking her heart and deserting her to drown in a pool of tears and confusion. Contact was reinitiated with new hope, but it was a false gesture. With only a month to go before he would move back to Denmark to complete his studies, it felt like make or break time. But the chance had already passed. The friendship was awkward, side stepping the central subject. It was as if they had become strangers, foreigners in the friendship. They did not talk as long as before; the honesty had died. Van moved back to Denmark, and she supposed they might keep in touch, but the phone calls and emails soon fizzled out. It all seemed rather pointless now, anyway. She had broken the rule of best friends, and had paid the fee for ignoring the contract. Your love has left and there's no best friend to cheer you up. He had finally discovered the desperate side of her personality and departed. Of all the girls in the world, she was the last one he needed.

She mourned and cried through the summer holidays in preparation for her final year. Reason revived itself eventually, and she began to see that he really was the wrong kind of person for her. He had done her a great favour in refusing her. But the fear of having no misery to cling to hit and she relapsed for another two months before finally getting over him and focussing on her studies. A broken heart was nothing new; everyone suffered from this in life.

On her last night in her student residence, she found the old half-written story about the angry Finn on her computer. She curled up in the chair and read the snippets of a fictional life set as a poor disguise for her old friend Van. She wondered what he was doing now. Whatever he was doing, he would be doing it with that same pig-headed attitude and the same grit of the teeth. Determination and aggression. Don't give an inch. Wherever he was.

For Mercedes, however, he was now in the trash can. Fact or fiction, enough time had passed by to leave this as a memory parallel to something she might have seen on television a few months ago. And there were better things out there to be had.

Part Twelve
The Secret in the Shell

Jo's reflection intermingled with the rushing dry countryside on the other side. The train carriage rattled; paint peeling off in the sun-baked heat. Jimanac was far behind, somewhere up the twist of metal rails cutting through the flat, wild country of dry steppes, cacti speckled over the plains like strange organic gothic cathedrals to the sun.

In the train compartment the air was stale and gently steaming. Jo got up and dragged the window down. Wind whipped her in the face as the dirty glass panel barrier was removed. The sound of motion roared in through the open hole.

Slumping back into her seat, she glanced across at the nurse who was sat beside her. She was a figureless, ageless woman seemingly void of a personal life; at least it was impossible to imagine her with one. She had a motherly way of talking and patience that had never been broken. She was currently engrossed in a nursing magazine. The page was open at an article on lancing boils: an in depth look at the history of boils, various treatments depending on country and body part, and some of the worst recorded cases. Complete with full colour pictures.

Jo shuddered and looked away from the magazine. She did not know how people managed to work in health care. The human body in all its rotting glory made her shy back into the shadows. Sickness, excretions, leakages and other manifestations made her feeble minded, incapable. People had expected her to go into some branch of the health care, considering the route her life had taken, but she had shunned all their ideas and taken history instead. It was a much safer alternative: just her and a library full of dusty books.

The nurse snapped her magazine shut and looked at her watch. "We should get there in about quarter of an hour. I am looking forward to this. I haven't been to the coast since last September. And it's such a lovely day today."

"I haven't been to the coast since I was six." Jo commented idly. "It was the last trip I made with mama before..." she faltered, glancing awkwardly across at her mother who was sat opposite her. "Well, you know, the breakdown."

"Then it's about time we all took a trip to the sea side," declared the nurse, stuffing the magazine into her large, shapeless bag. "It does them a world of good," she continued in an authoritative tone as if Letitia wasn't there. "Get them out into the fresh air, a change of scene. Much better than staring at the same four walls."

If Letitia was listening, she didn't show it. If she comprehended the discussion, it didn't register in her conscious brain. She sat like a wooden doll, complete with awkward crazy carved grin, and rocked with the repetitive motion of the train. Her frizzy black hair was bunched up high in two pigtails, the hair exploding out like atom-bomb mushrooms. She always screamed if she did not have her pigtails, stomping her feet on the grey linoleum floor of the mental hospital like a five-year-old. Essentially she was a five-year-old, and a damned confused one at that. A five-year-old locked up in the tall, once elegant body of a forty something woman.

Jo couldn't really remember her mother as an adult. There had been the trip to the beach of course, when she had been six. Things had been all right then, but strangely her memories of a sane, traditionally adult mother were missing, as if she had gone to the beach on her own. By the time she was nearing eight the doctors were in the flat trying to get some sense from Letitia. They gave up and had her institutionalised. Jo went to live with her aunt.

The train pulled into the station and the three women waited a couple of minutes for the other passengers to get off before they attempted to leave. Letitia was very meek and compliant this morning, allowing her daughter to take her by the hand and lead her down the corridor to the exit. Dressed in her flat brown sandals and simple white dress that looked like a rectangle with sleeves, she descended from the train carriage onto the platform. The air smelt of sea salt.

Jo was used to looking after her mother. Other little girls had received baby dolls for Christmas, Jo had received Letitia. Perhaps received was the wrong word, but despite the lacking of traditional family life and the moments of woe without a steady role model, there was something very sincere and innocent about Letitia, something that was reminiscent of a gift.

Her mother's breakdown had taken about a year to take its full effect and grind her brain down to child-like pulp. Jo had dealt with the tears, the tantrums, the attacks and the days after when Letitia lapsed back into adult hood, suffering amnesia and having no idea why someone had painted rainbows in crayon in her bedroom. She blamed Jo, who was at the age for such mischief, but subsequent farm yard animals on the ceiling seemed just a little out of her daughter's reach.

Even when Letitia had passed the point of no return, Jo continued to look after her infantile parent. They had managed happily for two months before the previously mentioned aunt called by unexpectedly and realised what was going on. Social Services were promptly notified.

Before she was ten, Jo had practical experience of nursing care, psychiatrics and the complicated system of social services. Everyone expected her to grow up and work with mental health care; after all, she had such a deep understanding of mental illness, and she did not judge. But Jo shuddered from bodily contact with strangers and the thought that there were hundreds, perhaps even thousands more like her mother out there terrified her.

They bought take-away fish suppers for lunch and sat in a discrete corner of the town park eating their food. Letitia needed two serviettes; one tucked in her collar and one on her lap, and had to be spoon-fed. Jo watched the nurse feed her mother, talking to her like a baby and wondered for a moment why she was here. She stopped by the hospital every other day to visit Letitia – more visits than any of the other patients had. Girls at university usually slept late and went to parties; spent afternoons in the park gossiping with friends or lying in the sunshine reading books. Jo just didn't seem to be able to relax.

Standing on the beach, the nurse holding her bag by her side like a suitcase, Jo with her arms folded, they watched Letitia run joyfully down the white sands to the sea. Her arms were stretched out wide as if she was trying to take off, her mouth rounded open to a black hole, the wind streaming through her hair. She splashed straight into the frothy water as a wave rolled over and came crashing to the shore.

"And the waves roar!" Letitia boomed, flinging her hands up to the sky.

Jo's emotionless face cracked. "Why does she have to be like this?"

The nurse glanced across at her. "I thought the doctors explained after her trial period. She broke down…"

"I know what the doctors said," groaned Jo. "But why did she have to break down? Is her mind really that weak? Is anyone's mind that weak?" Her hands were tightening to fists as her questions poured forth. "What is the point with all of this?"

The nurse smiled sympathetically. "There is no answer, dear. It's just life. Some people have it easier than others. You've just got to try and make the best of what you get."

If you can manage it, Jo thought bitterly, watching Letitia crouch down in the sea foam. The doctors had said that Letitia was unable to cope with real life – the world of an adult and all its responsibilities, and had thus reverted to a child-like state. They doubted she could be brought out of this state. Letitia had just given up.

With wet sand creeping up in-between her toes, Letitia reached out and picked up a shell. It was a large conch shell, ripples of pink tone across the smooth inner surface, the edges battered smooth by the sea.

Jo watched her from a distance. When she had last come here with her mother they had collected shells. Letitia had said that you could hear the voice of the ocean in the shells, if only you held them to your ear and opened your mind to the voices. Jo had tried but all she could hear was a sound like the wind. It was probably just her inner ear amplified. Perhaps Letitia had already been loosing it even then.

Letitia held the shell cautiously to her ear and fell silent. She remained in that position for a good few minutes before smiling to herself, considering over what she had just heard. "So that's what it's all about."

Lovers of Old Films
Ophelia Finsen

Fresh from university and eager for the rest of his life, Edward Gable moves to York to start a position in a graduate training scheme. And whilst real life may not meet his expectations, the building he moves into can more than compensate for the lack of excitement. Certainly everyone is friendly and helpful, but there are secrets no one wants to talk about – and if you find yourself living in a building with Sophia Loren, you know something out of the ordinary is going to happen.

Ever wanted to be your idol?
You might want to think again…

Society of Lost Causes
Ophelia Finsen

In a small town in the Yorkshire Dales there is a select gathering known as the Society of Lost Causes. A gathering of eccentric and unknown people; people who feel that they or their work will have no consequence for the world. Until a murder without motive is committed in their small community, and three potential witnesses are drawn together permanently through the twist and turns of a crime scene and an organisation dedicated to remembering contemporary and historical oddities.

This is a tale of the joy of story-telling; of the fascination in the detail and the small curiosities of life that are there for anyone to find if they are only prepared to stop and listen.

www.ingramcontent.com/pod-product-compliance
Lightning Source LLC
Chambersburg PA
CBHW050818180626
46814CB00004B/1350